MW01131314

BOOKS BY TIM MCBAIN & L.T. VARGUS
Casting Shadows Everywhere
Fade to Black (Awake in the Dark #1)
Bled White (Awake in the Dark #2)

FADE TO BLACK

FADE TO
BLACK

TIM MCBAIN
L.T. VARGUS

SMARMY PRESS

FADE TO BLACK

- 1 -

Any minute now a hooded man will come barreling out of nowhere and kill me.

So that sucks.

I know this because it has happened six times before. I wake up in this alley, hung from a post by a piece of rope lashed to one ankle, tied in a hangman's knot. After several minutes of work, I pry my bonds free, and about thirty seconds after I hit the ground, this guy in a black hooded robe gives me a pretty bad case of death.

His hands are cold on my neck. And dry. I try to fight him, to claw at his eyes, but I can't reach, to scratch at his arms, but he's too strong. He's silent. I try to yell at him, but I manage more of a gurgle and some clicky noises. I don't even know what I'd say, I guess, but I can assure you that he seems like a real dick.

Everything goes all fuzzy and fades to gray, then black. I die, and then I go... someplace else, I guess.

I don't know. I can't remember that part just now.

Anyway, I guess I should try something different this time. I fold at the waist, my fingers picking at the knot while I think it over. I've tried running out of both ends of the alley. Tried fighting the guy.

All of these failed in spectacular fashion. I'll need to get creative this time.

There's really only one other option I can think of. I get the knot loose enough to slip my ankle free of the rope and plummet to the ground, landing on my feet which immediately slide out from under me to plant my lower back in a mud puddle.

Nice.

I hop up and pop the lid of a dumpster open and lift myself so I'm sitting on the lip. Flies circle near my face before returning to their bacteria buffet. I totter forward, my hands latching onto the metal sides to stop my momentum. My chest heaves in and out with a single deep breath. This may not be the best idea I've ever had, I suppose, but I'd rather avoid getting strangled, so what the hell? I plunge feet first into the pile of trash. I sink and bags shift to flop their limp weight on top of me. Garbage water squishes around me.

It's juicy as hell in here, and it smells like liquid ass.

I can't see the soft mass resting under my hands and knees, but if I had to guess? Dead dog.

I never get a look at his face. The hooded man, I mean. He somehow tucks back into the shadow under the hood. I can make out the outline of his chin, one corner of his wet mouth, but that's it.

For now all I can make out is a little light streaming between the sacks of waste above me and the aforementioned juicy odor. I wait. And wait. I consider poking my head out to breathe some semi fresh air, but I decide against it. It'd be dumb to submerge myself in putrid liquid like this only to get strangled for trying to breathe oxygen that smells like 90% sewage instead of 300% sewage. I can tough it out.

After petting the dog for a few minutes, I hear footsteps rush into the alley and hesitate. This is it. I feel like I finally appreciate what the cliché "when the shit hits the fan" means, too, because in the dumpster it smells exactly like someone threw a bunch of logs into spinning blades.

The footsteps creep closer, and there's a sloshing sound. I picture his foot sinking ankle deep into a pothole turned mud puddle and almost laugh. Maybe I'm covered in piss and dead dog juice, but he has a wet foot now!

He scampers past the dumpster, pausing at the end of the alley before moving on.

Interesting. This is a new development in our game of cat and guy choking cat. As much as I want to get the eff out of this dumpster, I should wait here a moment longer before I move out. Give him some time to create some distance between us.

I stand, and my head emerges from the debris just enough to get a peek at the end of the alley.

Nothing.

I hold my breath and listen for a moment.

Nothing.

It suddenly strikes me that it really is nothing. No cars going by. No pedestrians around. This seems important, but I can't think of why just now.

I pull myself out of the dumpster, but my foot catches on the rim, and I splat face first on the asphalt.

"Fuck!" I say.

It occurs to me immediately that I've said this altogether too loudly considering I am trying to, you know, not get murdered. I bring my hand away from my cheek bone, and it's bloody with a bunch of sand stuck in it.

I look up, and there he is, standing at the end of the alley. Just standing there.

I try to think of a name or something to call him, but none of them seem dramatic enough to do this scenario justice. I mean, what can you say to the guy that's about 30 seconds away from snuffing your life out for the seventh damn time? Did I already mention that this guy is a real jerk?

I run. I reach the other end of the alley and bank to the left and keep going. My feet pound the pavement, and I can hear his footsteps echoing mine, drawing closer.

I take another sharp left at the intersection, hoping to gain a little ground with the change of direction.

For the first time I realize how gray everything seems. The sky. The buildings around me. The street. The sidewalk. It doesn't seem right. This place isn't normal. I try to remember what I was doing before I woke up in this alley, but I can't.

I cut left again at the next intersection, I guess out of habit at this point.

His footsteps are much louder now. Close. I sneak a peek over my shoulder just in time to see his outstretched hand reach for the back of my collar. I juke away from him and veer left. He follows, reaches out again.

Just as I think I should probably look where I'm going, I slam into the dumpster and drop to the ground like a bag of sand. I guess that's what four left turns gets you. My fall is so fast, he can't slow down in time and kicks my head, which sends him – Wait, let me rephrase that. I heroically place my head in the perfect spot to trip him, which sends him sprawling into the same mud puddle I fell in earlier.

I can literally see some stars from the cranium kick, but you should see the other guy. He's soaked!

I pull myself to my feet. I'm too wobbly to run, so I lean against the dumpster.

Aw, what the hell? I crawl back into the dumpster, face first this time. If this guy wants to kill me, fine, but let's just say he's probably going to have to touch a dead dog to do it.

I hear him move toward the trash bin, and then there's a familiar metallic sound that I can't quite place. After a very brief lull, I hear what sounds like him jabbing his hand into the garbage. He jabs again and then three more times in rapid succession.

Except I see his hand plunge through the garbage about three inches from the tip of my nose, and it's weird because his hand looks exactly like the blade of a ridiculous combat knife. Like if you had just killed a dinosaur, you would use this thing to skin it. Otherwise, it'd be too big to have any practical purpose I can think of.

So this is yet another new development. He's wielding a knife.

How wonderful.

I watch the knife jabs work their way away from me to the other end of the dumpster and then start their way back. I know I shouldn't move, that if I move he'll see exactly where I am. But once he's within about a foot and a half of me, I can no longer resist the urge to put the dead dog on top of me for protection. Before I can even lift the carcass, though, the knife skims my ear and enters that ball of muscle that connects the neck and shoulder.

This is the opposite of awesome.

He pulls the knife out, and without thinking about it, I lay back, I guess to shrink away from my attacker. I feel the wet warmth surge along the back of my neck. Things suddenly seem quiet, and I realize that I must have been screaming and just stopped.

The knife plunges through the trash once again, this time sinking into my torso two inches lower than my sternum, that soft space between the ribs. I grab his hands around the handle of the knife to try to hold the blade in so he can't keep at it, but he yanks it away without any real trouble.

The place where the knife was in my belly feels empty. A little cold. Like if you hold your mouth open and let the cool air touch everything in there, except a lot more painful.

I really need to figure out how I got here. Who just wakes up in alley that's all empty and shit? Hanging upside down by the foot? Someone must have put me here, I guess, but who? And why? And how do I even keep coming back? Who resurrects in this day and age?

I think I am in shock. Like now, I am out on the asphalt again. I guess he must have pulled me out of the dumpster. I don't know.

It's getting hard to keep my eyes open, and everything is a little blurry around the edges. I see the hooded man swing back into focus, and I realize that he's completely soaked. His robe looks like he's been rolling around in mud. It's a mess.

So that's good.

- 2 -

The first thing that drifts into my consciousness is some soft rock song. It sounds like it's playing far away. I don't know what it's called, but I know I've heard it before.

It blows.

The next thing I'm aware of is a warm breeze tickling my forehead in steady bursts.

"His eyelids are fluttering," a voice says.

Now, this voice is entirely too close to my face. It does not sound like the voice of someone you want close to your face. It sounds like the voice of a guy with a mustache that eats a lot of spaghetti, and it sounds like he's close enough to smear marinara on my cheek with a simple flick of the tongue.

When I first open my eyes, however, it's too bright to make out more than a silhouette hovering over me. I manage to keep my eyes open for a fraction of a second, but I'm left with more questions than answers. Am I in a hospital? Is this a doctor?

I clutch at my belly, but there's no bandage or any other sign of a knife wound.

"I think he's waking up," the voice says.

A murmur of other voices respond. There have to be at least 15 other people gathered nearby. OK, so that seems like a lot for a hospital room, and thinking it over a moment, the mustache voice doesn't sound all that educated.

And then the smell hits me. The warm breeze I've felt on my forehead? Smells like Funyuns. To be more specific, it smells exactly like Funyun breath. So I guess Dr. Funyun is mouth-breathing on my face.

"Are you awake, buddy?" he says.

"Yes."

I open my eyes just in time to see the guy wheel around to face all the ladies standing in a semi-circle around me here in the u-scan aisle at the supermarket, Meijer to be precise.

"He said 'yes,'" he says.

"We can hear him," an old lady clutching a tabloid to her chest says. Her voice sounds like she smokes tubes of actual tar instead of cigarettes.

The man turns back to face me. I sense right away that the grin plastered on his face is genuine. Also, I was right about the mustache, a black Tom Selleck style flecked with gray.

"Name's Glenn Floyd," he says, holding his hand out for me to shake.

"I'm Jeff Grobnagger," I say.

I sit up, and he claps me on the shoulder instead of a handshake. One of those hard shoulder claps usually reserved for awkward encounters between gym teachers and students.

"You scared me, man," he says. "I haven't seen somebody fish out like that since the time Ricky brought a nitrous tank to the party shack back in college."

He lifts the navy blue baseball cap off his head and runs his fingers through his hair.

"Fish out?" I say.

"Oh yeah," he says. "You were floppin' around like a fish, buddy. Trying to bite the floor and stuff. It was wild. Musta been one of them grand mal seizures or something, right?"

A couple of the ladies behind him nod gravely.

A woman strides up on us with a cell phone pressed to her ear. She's wearing pleated front khakis and a fancier version of the Meijer polo shirt, so I take her as some kind of manager.

"Are you feeling all right, sir?" she says.

"Yes, I'm fine."

"I'm glad to hear that. We've called an ambulance, so we'll need you to sit tight until they get here," she says.

I get to my feet.

"What? No," I say. "I'm not getting in any ambulance."

I detect a hint of panic in my voice, so I try to do a nonchalant shoulder shrug to conceal it. Like "I'm not getting in any ambulance *because I'm cool.* Not terrified in the slightest." Glenn squints and gives a nod of approval. I think the Meijer lady buys it as well.

"Sir, it's store policy for us to have you wait here until medical professionals can assist you," she says. "This is in the best interest of your well being as well as our store's insurance purposes."

"Well, I happen to have a very strict policy regarding me not going to the hospital."

Glenn chuckles.

"Oh, man," he says.

I hate to toot my own horn, but I'm getting the distinct sense that Glenn is very impressed with me. Also, I lied earlier. I love tooting my own horn.

I turn toward the door, moving quickly.

"Grobnagger," Glenn says, running to catch up with me. "You almost forgot your wheat grass… and these."

He shoves a little plastic planter of wheat grass and my sunglasses into my hands. So I guess I was here to buy wheat grass. Not sure. I'm guessing the sunglasses popped off when I fell.

I slide them back on. I pretty much always wear sunglasses – inside, outside, daytime, nighttime - doesn't matter. I like to feel covered up, I guess. Plus it's comforting to see the world through lenses that mute all the harshness out there. It's like having a dimmer switch for reality.

For a second I think maybe the old man who says hi and bye to everybody is going to try to physically stop me from leaving the store with some kind of crazy old man neck grip or something. Instead he just tries to guilt me into staying with a dirty look and a slow motion head shake. I cross through the doorway and step away from the building.

In the parking lot, a shriek distracts me – my eyes lock onto a young couple loading groceries into the back of a Hyundai Sonata. The girl has long, scrawny limbs and an equally long face like someone grabbed her by head and foot and stretched all of her out when the bones were still soft when she was an infant. Still pretty, though. The guy has a low brow and muscular legs that suggest a life spent lifting heavy objects for both work and pleasure.

She pushes him in the chest, and he totters backward. Then she squeals in glee as he does a Frankenstein like stalk after her with raised arms. He grips and lifts her in a sort of bear hug, her face going all red in laughter as her frail fists pound at his chest.

Eh…

She could do better.

As I move through the lot, shards of memory start piecing together what all has happened to me here. I had just rung up my wheat grass in the u-scan lane when I overheard Glenn next to me.

"Excuse me, miss," he said to the cashier standing about 15 feet away. "This item won't scan."

He shook a can of Hershey's syrup at her. I watched as the cashier made eye contact with him but didn't help, didn't acknowledge his query at all, in fact, instead turning and walking in the other direction.

"What the fuck?!" Glenn said in a gravelly falsetto that was almost quiet enough to be to himself.

I almost laughed, but he immediately started talking to me.

"Do your cats eat that wheat grass?" he said.

He pointed at the wheat grass.

"That's what I'm about to find out," I said.

"It's supposed to be really good for them," he said. "My cats loved it at first, and now they won't touch the stuff. Figures, right?"

I remember that I tried to respond to this, but it was like my mouth didn't work. First no sound came out even though I was telling it to, and then once I could speak, it was all garbled into stuttering nonsense.

"Whoa. You alright?" Glenn said.

And then everything faded to black. The next thing I knew I was strung up by my left foot in an oddly gray alley.

See, a few months ago I started having these seizures. Sometimes I'm out for a few minutes. Sometimes it's hours. They keep getting more frequent. Actually, the last two were less than a week apart. And each seizure is a one way ticket to strangle city.

Are they just dreams, though? The stranglings in the alley, I mean. Seizure dreams or something? That would make the most sense, of course, but I don't think I believe it. Not all the way, at least.

I don't know.

I move beyond the parking lot and onto the sidewalk. A flame broiled smell emitting from Burger King engulfs this region. It always makes me feel dumb that I think it smells pretty good, and then I remember that some guys in a lab off of the New Jersey turnpike worked very hard to make sure it was an odor I would like.

Yum.

A car with what sounds like no muffler at all pulls up next to me and slows to an idle. I hear the whir of the window going down, and the sound of a familiar voice.

"Hey Grobnagger. Want a ride?" he says. "You probably shouldn't be out walking after your… uh… incident back there."

It's Glenn.

I'm about to say no when I hear the siren in the distance. I picture the old lady releasing the tabloid from her chest to point me out and a couple of hooded paramedics tying me down to a stretcher and forcing me into the back of the ambulance. And though I know this won't actually happen, I just want to get out of here.

"Yeah, alright," I say.

I climb into the passenger seat of Glenn's 2002 Ford Explorer. It's sort of a purpley-red with a pink rear bumper. Bright pink.

"I live close," I say as I close the door. "Like seven blocks from here."

"Oh, that's cool," he says.

I notice that he's sporting some ridiculous wrap around Oakleys that look they were minted in about 1988. I can't say for sure, but I like to think that they are the Jose Canseco signature model.

"You know the Park Terrace Apartments?" I say. "On Kendall?"

"Yep."

"That's where we're headed."

"You got it, buddy."

The oldies station Glenn is listening to is playing "My Baby Does The Hanky Panky." He cranks up the stereo, and we make our way in the general direction of my apartment, the ambulance rushing past us about thirty seconds into the journey.

I watch the city out of the window. All of the grass looks brown and frizzy because it hasn't rained in a while. McDonald's cups and hubcaps huddle with road kill in clusters on the side of the road. The chimney at KFC spews smoke that looks like it's about to congeal into a solid black object in the sky.

And suddenly I realize that we passed the turn to my apartment a while ago.

"You missed my street," I say.

Glenn pushes his sunglasses down to the tip of his nose and regards me.

"I need to swing by to feed my cats and give them their medication if that's cool," he says. "Then I'll get you home."

"Well," I say. "OK."

He pushes the sunglasses back up.

"My oldest, Leroy, has had real bad acid reflux for a while now. I have to feed him small quantities multiple times a day and watch him like a hawk to make sure he doesn't try to steal the other cats' food."

I nod.

"If left to his own devices, he scarfs that extra food and upchucks everywhere."

"Right," I say.

"Thing is, I don't even mind cleaning up the cat vomit. Not really. It just kills me that he's tearing up his esophagus and can't keep any food down, and the poor guy is still hungry after all that, you know?"

"Yeah."

"It ain't right."

After several more blocks of contemplating feline digestive issues in silence, we arrive at Glenn's house, a bungalow that looks in better repair than I had anticipated. I guess I don't know what I expected, really, maybe empty Funyun bags rolling about the lawn like tumbleweed or something.

Glenn cracks the driver's side door open, and then swivels his head at me, trying to force me to lock eyes with those damn Oakleys. I don't take the bait, keeping my gaze focused on the corner of a road map sticking out of the glove box.

"I'll just wait in the car," I say.

"You're probably going to want to come in," he says. "This can take like 20 minutes if Leroy's in an ornery mood and Patches pecks at her Friskies the way she often does."

"It's fine," I say. "I don't mind waiting."

"I have to insist that you come on in, Grobnagger," he said. "I'll fix you something to eat and drink, and you can watch me wrangle these cats."

We're quiet for a time.

"Listen, I'm going to feel like a real dick face if you just wait out here," he says.

"OK," I say, not quite believing the words coming out of my mouth. "I guess."

I open the door and follow him in. I think maybe he had me at "dick face."

Inside, the house is spotlessly clean. There are little Martha Stewart style decorative displays everywhere. Elaborate center pieces. Vases of flowers. Baskets of fruit.

"Do you live here by yourself?" I say.

"Yeah," he says. "Just me and these fuzz bags."

He gestures at the black cat winding around his legs, tilting its head to push its face against the leg of his pants.

"That's Leroy. Leroy, this is Jeff Grobnagger," he says. "But yeah, this is my bachelor pad. Got divorced from the Crypt Keeper four years ago. Thank God. Our daughter is grown, and…"

He trails off, which seems out of character. He seems less the type to trail off into thoughtful silence and more the type to emphasize his point by spraying flecks of Funyun while stating it.

"Anyhow," he says. "I'll get you something to chow on."

I consider telling him that I'm not hungry, but I say nothing. He pulls some Tupperware containers out of the fridge and starts plopping stuff on a plate.

"You mind if I ask how old you are?" he says.

"I'm 27."

"Really?" he says. "You look younger than that. Shit, you could pass for a high school kid."

"That's what people tell me."

"What's your secret?"

I scratch my chin.

"Well," I say. "I avoid stressful shit as much as possible. Keeps you young."

"Interesting," he says. "Real interesting. What kind of stressful stuff do you mean, though?"

"Worrying about money. Working a real job. Talking to people. Stuff like that."

Glenn doesn't say anything for a long moment. He just raises his eyebrows. He puts something in the toaster oven, but his torso shields me from getting a good look at it.

"Fair enough," he says finally.

"How old are you?" I say, not wanting the conversation to stall on such a sour note.

"I am 56 years young," he says. "I know what you're thinking, too. '56? Shit, you could pass for 54 easy, dude.'"

I laugh a little.

"Yeah," I say. I sometimes don't know what to say after people make a joke, so I just say "Yeah."

"Here," he says.

He places a plate piled with Caribbean jerk chicken sauced with mango cilantro salsa, fried plantains, and some kind of black bean and rice concoction that seems to be held together with cheese that is effing delicious.

"Thanks," I remember to say a couple of bites in. "This is tasty as hell."

"I like the leftover chicken better cold, but if you want I can heat it up for you," he says. "Else wise, the four legged lords of the manor await their meal."

He bows at the waist and rotates his hand in a florid gesture between us as though he's a servant bidding my royal leave. I continue to mow the food while he goes about feeding his four cats. It might be the best plate of food I've ever eaten.

He's still standing over the feasting cats when I finish my meal. I guess he's been waiting until I was done to re-establish our conversation as he asks a question seconds after I swallow the last bite.

"Where do you work?" he says.

"I don't," I say.

"Oh?" he says.

"I made a bunch of money playing poker online a few years ago," I say. "I live off of that."

"That's awesome," he says. "So you don't play anymore?"

I shake my head.

"A few years ago, it was so easy," I say. "A bunch of people that didn't know what they were doing flocked to online poker sites and basically wound up letting people like me extract the money from their accounts. The government shut a lot of shit down, though, so a lot less people are playing poker these days. The ones that still do play are pretty good."

A piece of rice is stuck in my molars, and I work at dislodging it with my tongue.

"Plus, I don't have the same drive to make money that I did back then."

Glenn tilts his head and looks at me through halfway opened eyes.

"Seems like it'd be stressful, though," he says.

"Nope," I say. "Poker is a game, you know? And playing online, it almost doesn't feel real. I know I'm up against real people, but there's no confrontation. I just sit alone, stare at a screen and click a mouse button. The chips I'm risking don't even seem like real money. I get the feeling of risk - the exhilaration - but it's not real. It's just a game."

"I guess I can see that," he says.

"Sometimes it starts to feel too real, and I clam up, go on little losing streaks. That's when I have to take a break," I say. "But normally, it's so not real to me that I'm pretty relaxed. I just antagonize the other players with aggression until they start making mistakes."

Glenn laughs.

"It's all artificial, though," I say. "The conflict isn't real. I win because I have a combination of less fear and more discipline than my opponents. But I don't have those traits in the real world. I have them in the game."

I'm not sure what has gotten into me to start ranting like this. We fall silent for a moment.

"So are you epileptic?" he says.

"You mean because of the seizure?" I say. "I don't know."

"You don't know?" he says. "What the hell do you mean you don't know?"

"I've never been to a doctor about it," I say.

I try out the cool shrug again, but Glenn is not having it this time.

"Are you kidding?" he says. "How long have you been having seizures?"

"Six or seven months, I guess."

"How many times total?"

"7."

"Were you rendered unconscious all 7 times?"

"Yes."

"Jesus, buddy. That is what doctors would call 'alarming.'"

"Going to the doctor is stressful. I told you. I don't do stressful shit."

"You know what's stressful? Dying is pretty stressful," he says. "If you don't go to the doctor, you might do that instead."

"We'll see, I guess," I say.

Glenn takes off his hat and splays his fingers through his hair again. I guess that must be one of his go to moves.

"Do you ever even think about seeing a doctor?" he says. "You must."

"I think about it, but then I think about playing video games, and that generally sounds more fun."

He takes my plate and rinses it off in the sink.

"Do you dream?" he says. "When you have one of your seizures, I'm saying. Do you dream when you have a seizure?"

"Yep."

I'm so thankful for the opportunity to get off the topic of doctors that I tell Glenn everything. The hanging. The strangling. Every detail in between.

He is the first person I've told any of this to.

When I finish, he doesn't say anything for a long time. He just looks at me.

"You're not into occult stuff, are you?" he says.

"No."

"I didn't figure," he says. "Wait here."

He comes back with a photo album, a black leather bound

book with a weird silver symbol etched onto the cover, and a metallic sphere in contrasting hues of maroon and gold. Of course, I want to get a look at the sphere first, but he sets it aside. Instead, he riffles through the pages of the photo album until he finds the proper place and sets it in front of me.

"This is my daughter, Amity," he says. "These are the most recent pictures I have. Maybe six or eight months old."

He points to a girl in her late 20s with dark hair and wide set eyes. She is pretty, but she looks sad in all of the photos.

"She's missing," he says. "Nobody has heard from her in 36 days. Not her friends. Not me. Not even the Crypt Keeper, whom she talks to daily."

He places the weird black book in front of me.

"I got the landlord to let me into her apartment where I found this," he says. "It was hidden in the furnace vent next to her bed. Nothing else in the apartment seemed amiss."

I open the book, but it's printed in some ornate looking language I've never seen before.

Glenn picks up the sphere and balances it in his palm between us for a moment before he finally hands it over.

"This I found in one of those long term storage lockers at the airport," he says. "The key was in her top dresser drawer."

Holding the sphere in my hands, I realize it's covered in symbols. Hieroglyphics, maybe. The body is maroon and three gold rings run around the sides and can be rotated around, perhaps to line up the symbols? I tilt the sphere to get a look at all sides, and I hear a ball bearing rolling about inside as I move it. I also spot a gold button on one side that depresses.

"Is it a puzzle?" I say.

"No clue," Glenn says. "I did some Google searches but all

that came up was stuff about the Lament Configuration or LeMarchand's box – the box from the movie Hellraiser."

"Weird," I say.

I twist the rings a few times and press the button. Nothing happens.

"Amity was always into weird stuff, morbid stuff," he says. "She loved horror movies when she was a toddler and started reading Aleister Crowley books when she was 9 or 10. It went on from there. But I never thought her curiosity about these things could actually hurt her."

I don't know what to say. As I open my mouth to tell him I'm sorry to hear all of this, he goes on.

"Like I said, I found no information about the sphere, and reading the book wasn't possible, of course. Asking around, however, I found out that she'd been hanging around some local groups that claim to be into magic and occult stuff. Not devil worshippers exactly, but you could call them cults. Maybe not as organized as a full on kool-aid cult, but you wouldn't be far off. I figured realistically we were talking about con men, maybe a leader assuming some messiah like role to get women and money. Maybe a group that talked her into isolating herself from her family for the good of their phony religion, though I wouldn't think Amity would be susceptible to something like that. I guess anything is possible."

He pauses a moment and drums his fingers on the counter.

"But what you described in your seizure dream? It's a lot like the stuff both of these groups write about. Involuntary astral projection and a series of spiritual tests where failure ends in figurative death. The worthy initiate respawns and tries again until they pass the test and move on to the next."

21

I swallow in a dry throat.

"Thing is, these guys train for years to try to trigger these astral projections and spiritual tests. They train and train and basically nothing happens. I was actually surprised about how frank they were about that aspect of it on their websites and in their newsletters. I figured there'd be all kinds of outlandish claims, but they're pretty straight forward that none of them have achieved much in terms of paranormal experiences or enlightenment or whatever. They just keep trying."

I run the back of my hand over my lips.

"I think mine are just dreams," I say.

A pained look forms on his face and fades.

"Maybe you're right," he says. "But I'm a desperate man nonetheless. I would do or try anything to find my daughter. And my gut says you could help me with that."

I don't avoid his eye contact this time. I stare straight at him.

"I think we met for a reason. Will you help me?" he says.

"No," I say without hesitation.

An edge creeps into his voice, an anger.

"Why?" he says.

"Look, it sucks about your daughter," I say, "But I don't know you or her. And you obviously don't know me. Cause if you did, you'd know that I wouldn't stick my neck out for the people I do know, let alone a stranger. All I want from the world is to be left alone, ok? That's all. I just want to serve out my time in peace, as much of it as I can find, anyway. Is that so goddamn much to ask?"

His eyes whirl away from me and look to the floor. The silence lasts for what feels like a long time.

"Fair enough," he says.

- 3 -

Glenn offered to give me a ride home, but I insisted I'd walk. I'm not sure if that was out of pride or a fear that I'd somehow get roped into like six more stops along the way. Anyway, I'm walking, so, of course, it's sprinkling now.

I hurry along, hoping that the real rain is a ways off yet. I don't know this part of the city very well. Maybe it's just the dark and the wet, but it seems shitty. A liquor store with duct tape crisscrossing the front window takes shape in the distance, illustrating my point. The majority of the businesses around here seem to advertise that they buy gold, have guns for sale or both. And the locals I've happened across seem like the types that traded all of their gold for guns some time ago.

A man puts his arm around a woman on the sidewalk across the street. She nuzzles against him, like he can keep her out of the rain.

Good luck with that.

I arrive at an intersection and jab a finger at the crosswalk button just as the rain really picks up. Rivulets of water gush down from the side of Lucky's Pawn Shop next to me, pelting the cement with a slap and sizzle. I'm kept partially dry under the awning, but the spray from the ground mists one side of my face. The water seems especially cold.

Yelling down the block catches my attention. I look up to

see a prostitute standing in the doorway of a building to keep out of the wet. A man berates her from the sidewalk.

"I don't give a got damn. Get out there," he says. "Walk between the rain drops if you gotta, but get me that money."

She struts out onto the block, some sass in her walk, which seems extra sad to me somehow since she is doing exactly what the pimp told her to. It's the sass walk of the powerless.

Though the light next to me remains green, a black Lincoln pulls up and stops. The passenger door opens, and a large man in a suit steps out. At first, I think maybe he just has some gold to sell, but he seems pretty focused on me. The world is really sucking at the whole leaving me alone thing lately.

"Ms. Babinaux will see you now," he says.

Now, I have no idea who Ms. Babinaux is. Seems to be of French descent. That's all I've got. My guess, of course, is that she has something to do with one of the groups slash cults that Glenn mentioned, though how they might know about me and my seizures, I couldn't say. Still, my instincts say it's best not to tip off my knowledge or lack thereof. I'm guessing they already know the French part, anyway.

"I assume she's in back," I say.

He tilts his head forward to say yes.

"Well, if she has eyes, I'm sure she will see me," I say.

I give a mock wave and smile at the general vicinity of the backseat of the car.

"Here I am. It's me!" I say in a squeaky voice.

The guy snorts and then laughs. At first I think this is some form of sarcasm, but no. It's real laughter.

"Are you new at this?" I say. "Cause stoicism is like 50% of your job description. You're supposed to look imposing and be stoic. That's it. And you're totally effing it up."

"Just get in," he says, opening the door.

I think about running at first, but this would be a good way to get out of the rain and get home. I can't help but think that it'd be better if this were an actual limo, though, because in that case there would probably be beverages.

I climb into the backseat, which is fairly roomy but certainly not overly impressive. A dark haired woman raises her eyebrows at me. She is slender with facial features I associate with sophisticated rich ladies: sharp cheek bones, arched brows, high forehead. She smiles, but I can't get a read on whether it's a nurturing smile or a cold one.

"Nice to meet you, Mr. Grobnagger," she says, extending her hand.

Her hand feels tiny in mine, and somehow her handshake is dainty without seeming weak.

"Nice to meet you, too," I say. "You can call me Jeff."

It occurs to me that everything she does is hard to read. Like just now, she nods and tilts her head in a way that somehow simultaneously looks like a curious kitten and a buzzard about to peck a dead opossum's eyes out.

Which is it?

I don't know, dude.

"Well, this must be a very exciting time for you, so I'll try not to take up too much of your evening," she says.

"Not a problem," I say.

I turn to the driver.

"Do you know where Park Terrace Apartments are?" I say.

"Oh, we know where you live," she says.

"Great," I say.

It's not great, though. I can already imagine this infringing on my right to be left alone.

"We know quite a bit about you as a matter of fact. You wouldn't know this, but there's been a lot of talk about you in our… circles," she says. "I'm violating an agreement with a powerful ally just in speaking with you."

"Uh-huh," I say.

I came in here planning on giving no information, and I'm sticking with it.

"I'm afraid you're in some danger," she says.

I wait for her to elaborate, but she doesn't.

"And what might that entail?" I say.

"It's hard to say," she says. "Many people are invested in your endeavors. Some of them for less than savory reasons."

"I see," I say.

I don't actually see, though.

"Be very careful in who you deal with for the time being," she says.

I find this ironic considering she just ushered me into the backseat of a car with a stranger to have this discussion, but she goes on.

"One way or another, I think your would-be enemies will be contacting you soon, if they haven't already," she says.

I say nothing.

"I apologize for the vagueness. I'm unable to go into detail at this point for a variety of reasons. But do try to keep a low profile."

"You don't even know how low I want to keep this profile," I say.

We pull up to my apartment.

"I'll be in touch soon, and I should be able to share more with you at that time."

We shake hands, and I imagine how much more regal this all would have seemed if we were sitting across from each other in the back of a limo.

I lie in bed. I can't sleep. My thoughts keep returning to Glenn and his daughter. Yeah, I'm a dick that doesn't rescue damsels in distress. Whatever. My thoughts grow clear, though, as I guess they often do when I lie still for a long while.

Now, don't get me wrong. If I could press a button and save this guy's daughter, I would do that. I have nothing against him. He even seems like a nice guy. It's just that I don't get entangled with people. Not anymore. It only leads to pain, in my experience.

For years and years, I got dragged along by friends or family members, suckered into the middle of various dramas and conflicts. I was the sympathetic ear, the shoulder to cry on, the guy always there to help out. But as time went on, I realized that these were empty interactions. All of them.

I don't think most people want friends. They just want someone to listen when they talk. They don't want a connection, they want an audience. So as it dawned on me that this is what relationships meant to people, I felt sorry for them, but then it also meant that's all any relationship I had could be. Me feeling sorry for someone.

And it hurts to feel like that. Like you're not even an individual to anybody in a way, just the audience to witness their life and their thoughts. To know in your heart that no one really cares. It feels like the world is all one way streets that run away from you.

So I dropped out of all of it. No more friends. No more talking. I keep to myself. It's the code I live by. It keeps me safe.

Selfish? Maybe, but it's not so bad, I think. I mean, I don't hurt anybody. I don't bother anybody. I'm just alone.

In my time on my own, I've realized that I have no interest in reality. I don't really want to be part of it. To me, reality is going to funerals, going to hospitals. It's dead pets and cavities and the way all the possibilities disintegrate as you get older and older. It's nurturing relationships that can never go anywhere, disappointing people, being disappointed by people, various iterations of those same concepts over and over again.

I don't say this out of negativity. I'm not complaining about it. I say this out of acceptance. See, everyone is doing everything they can to escape reality all of the time. They're drinking and smoking weed, reading, watching TV, movies, sports, video games, collecting stuff, obsessing about celebrities, going to conventions, writing fiction and making up their own worlds. Basically every hobby is in some way an escape from reality. It is why everyone does everything they actually like doing.

For a while they get to disconnect and from the pain and death all around us.

Think about a funeral, anyway. For three days or so, a dead person is paraded around. They go through this rite of passage in getting their blood sucked out and some makeup smeared on. They get stuffed in a box and wheeled out for everyone to gawk at. None of this is actually for the dead person, of course. That person is gone. I guess it's for the people left behind. But how so? We gather in uncomfortable situations and stare at a corpse. We try to do them justice in words even though that's impossible, and then we bury them.

Maybe trying to make death a formal custom like a wedding means something to somebody, but it doesn't mean a goddamn thing to me. Maybe it helps someone out there deal with it to put on their Sunday best and pal around with distant relatives. Makes them feel like they aren't facing it alone or something.

To me, it's insane. It makes me feel worse. It makes me feel more alone.

See look, we put makeup on the body and a guy gave a speech. Now we can all feel better about it.

Bullshit. Fuck you.

So I take that premise that escaping reality is why everyone does everything and follow it to its conclusion: the only real and true reality is how I feel. I do not partake in any other forms of reality. I don't go to funerals. I don't go to hospitals. I don't go out to eat with people or feel obligated to make (or answer) social calls of any kind. Hell, I barely even talk to other people. I just keep to myself.

Like I said, I don't save damsels in distress.

Once you accept that escape is all you really want, though, things mostly get easier. It's a big relief in a way. You can say eff it and just try to have fun in whatever manner suits your personality. You don't have to feel guilty or get so anxious about anything. You can look at your time differently and try to find ways to relax and enjoy it and not get caught up in some imaginary chase that everyone else thinks is real.

You can let go.

I might have slept for a while in there but no longer. Now I'm watching the shadows of the rain drops streaking down the window, listening to the periodic cars rolling over the wet streets. I contemplate turning the light on to read for a while, but sometimes reading this late hurts my eyes.

This goes on for a while. Time works differently in the dark. It speeds up and slows down without letting me know, so I'm not sure how long I've been lying awake when I finally rise from the bed. As I step through the doorway, I can tell by the gray light creeping around the edges of the curtains that it's almost dawn.

My elbow brushes something odd as I move past the kitchen counter. It's cool with a little bristle to it. It almost feels like smooth hair. I flip on the light and squint while my eyes adjust. First, all I can see is a green blur in a square shape in the area where the elbow brushing transpired. As my pupils constrict, though, it comes into focus.

The wheat grass.

I set the planter on the floor and rub my index finger against my thumb above it to make an almost silent sound. To my cat, however, this sound is not even close to silent. I may as well have banged a gong. Mardy darts into the room, his eyes meeting mine for a second before he gazes upon the wheat grass and his expression goes half alarmed, half aroused. The gray cat stalks toward the grass, partially circling it and stopping short of it. His feet planted a safe distance away, he leans his face closer and closer until his nose and mouth make contact with the blades along the edge. His eyes narrow into half open slits.

As I'm watching this, waves of bad feelings rush over me.

My head gets heavy. My thoughts get tangled up. It's so subtle at first that I almost don't notice it, but it swells to the point that I feel like I'm about to topple over. I lower myself to the kitchen floor. The cat doesn't even notice. It's familiar, this feeling, but I can't quite place it.

I take a couple of deep breaths and start to gather my wits. I think the worst has passed.

And then everything goes black like someone flipped the switch on my brain.

I hear a creaking sound that somehow reminds me of a sailboat in the movies, like a pirate ship nearly motionless in the doldrums. Everything gets quiet again, and I start to drift back to sleep, but there it is again. The groan of rope straining against wood.

Oh.

That.

I open my eyes to find myself dangling upside down in the alley, rope corded around my ankle as per usual. I go to work untying myself, though I have some doubts as to the usefulness of this activity. Still, it's not like I have much else to do.

I hop down, keeping my feet under me this time. The soles of my shoes skim over the surface of the mud puddles. I move with some urgency. I know I have maybe 30 seconds worth of head start time.

I reach the downspout attached to the corner of the brick office building at the edge of the alley. My hands latch onto the aluminum, and I step up onto the brick wall – one foot and then the other. I dig my toes into the gaps between the bricks the best I can and push off from there, leaning back a little for balance. I bet I almost look like a guy rappelling down the face of a rock wall, but I'm going up. Not as rapidly as I'd like, but up all the same. I keep stepping and maintaining my chokehold on the downspout. I'm 10 or maybe 12 feet up now, but it's a big office building or something, and the roof is another 40 feet in front of me, I figure. Maybe more.

Something rattles beneath me. I glance down, and there he is. I would recognize that hood anywhere. I'm just out of his reach, so he tries to mount the wall the same way I have, but he can't seem to get any grip with his feet.

I can't watch him for long, though. I have to focus. Seeing him down there gives me a jolt of motivation or adrenalin, though. Maybe both. In any case, I'm making better progress now. I'm probably 25 feet off of the ground. My toes slip periodically, but I've gotten faster at recovering and moving forward.

Metal grunts and shrieks below. I look down, and he's no longer trying to climb the downspout. He's trying to rip it down. He jerks at the aluminum, and it gives a little like maybe the bracket is bending. The pained metallic wails assure me that the bracket is fighting back with all of its strength, at least. I thought the thing looked sturdier than most, but on the flipside, I can attest to the man's strength first hand. It's beyond human. There's a loud pop as one of the bolts gives out, and the aluminum tube suddenly moves more freely as he yanks on it.

I move faster, legs churning. The roof isn't so far off now.

Just as I gaze down again, he pulls the downspout free. A good 20 feet of aluminum tumbles toward the ground. I brace for this thing to rip out from under me, for the feeling of everything solid falling away. For a nanosecond, I even consider trying to grip the brick with my fingers or lunging for the gutter above.

Instead, nothing happens. The top half of the downspout is unaffected, the pair of brackets up here still being intact.

I laugh. I know I should keep moving before he starts throwing knives at me or something, but I can't help it. I stop a moment to chuckle and look down as his shoulders heave in frustration.

And then there are two more loud snaps in rapid succession as the top bracket gives. I'm falling. I'm still holding the downspout. Outwardly I'm screaming like a girl that has just seen Freddy Krueger crawl out of her closet, but inside I think about how you're supposed to land on your side when you fall a long way like this. How that is the only way for the body to absorb this kind of shock without serious injury, and that's if you're lucky. And just as I think about how I can try to rotate myself, I land flat on my back on the asphalt with a sound like two rams bashing their skulls into each other.

Two words burst into my head:

SHATTERED.

VERTABRAE.

My scream goes full falsetto. Pain shoots up and down me. It hurts everywhere. I can feel it in each of my teeth, and then it changes, and it feels overwhelmingly numb all over. So numb that it kind of hurts worse somehow, an overwhelming absence of feeling from the middle of my back down.

I realize that the blur moving toward me must be him, and I try to focus. I try to pay attention. I know time is almost up.

My scream fades to a whimper. I open my eyes wider. I suck in a big breath and hold it.

He kneels and puts his hand over my nose and mouth. It's like a mercy killing this time. All I can see is his jaw, but it's the clearest glimpse I've gotten yet. He looks younger than I figured. Slender. No trace of stubble. This is somehow more emasculating than ever. I'm getting murdered over and over by an oversized 8th grader.

Things are starting to get a little faded around the edges, so I employ my final breath. Though his hand muffles my words, I'm certain he can hear me:

"See you next time."

- 4 -

I wake on the kitchen floor with the cat hovering over my mouth, his whiskers tickling my top lip. I sit up, and Mardy trills before sauntering away. It looks like he tore into the wheat grass pretty good while I was out. Glenn would be pleased to hear that, I think.

I take a look around at the apartment, or what I can see of it from the floor anyway. Something feels off, but I kind of figure I just have post traumatic strangulation disorder at the moment. The kitchen light is still on. Elsewhere, sunlight streams in every crack it can find, illuminating the living room in half light. Everything appears in order. I stand and stretch. Repeated metaphysical deaths can cramp you right up if you don't stretch properly, so I try to stay limber. I open some blinds and flip off the kitchen bulb, trading artificial light for the real thing.

PTSD or not, waking up at home sure feels a lot better than waking up at the grocery store. I take a deep breath and let it out real slow. Even if I have no idea what the hell is wrong with me, I feel safe for the moment, and that's good enough.

I grind up some coffee beans and toast an apple cinnamon bagel - the breakfast of strangled champions. The coffee is some Sumatran kind I decided to try. Weirdly acidic and bright, but good as hell. I down a mug and pour another.

36

I pace back and forth across the ceramic tiles in the kitchen during the second mug. It's kind of a habit, I guess. I get a little caffeine in me, and I can't sit still. I swear walking gets your brain going in the right direction anyway, though. Gets the blood pumping to it.

My stimulated mind skips from topic to topic:

This coffee is effing great. It's expensive, but I think I'll have to stick with it. Can't imagine going back to the crappy stuff. I wonder if there are other kinds out there that are even better, though.

What am I going to do to that hooded bastard next time? I'm really running out of options. I should probably try to rip an eye out or something like that.

The wheat grass was a success. This is good. I wonder if it will stay that way or if Mardy will grow tired of it like Glenn's cats apparently did.

As soon as I think of Glenn's name, the image flashes in my head of the black book with the silver symbol he found in Amity's room. Not so great for reading, maybe, but it's a conversation piece. If you put a gun to my head and asked me to pick what language it's written in, I think I'd guess Orcish. Maybe Klingon. Wouldn't that be a kick in the sack, though? What seems like a legitimately mysterious and possibly evil book turns out to be some kind of Star Trek memorabilia?

At this point, my pacing takes me out into the living room. I walk to the far end of the apartment, and as I turn around, I see Mardy sniffing at the triangular opening between the front door and the hallway.

Wait.

There isn't supposed to be a triangular opening there.

I rush to the cat and scoop him up before he can abscond, placing him in the bedroom for the moment. The front door looks like someone took a battering ram to it while I was off in strangle land. The bottom hinge is busted off and the top hinge is barely holding on, so the door dangles at a 45 or so degree angle with the help of the security door chain, which I always keep latched. (Remember that thing about wanting to be left alone? Yeah.) There are cracks and splintered spots all over the place around the door frame. Even the steel door itself is dented pretty thoroughly. This took a lot of force.

Just as I squat to grip the sides of the door to try to finagle it back into the frame to keep the cat inside, glass behind me explodes. I don't think. I belly smack the floor. There are two more glassy bursts, and then everything goes quiet.

I look up and see broken windows behind me and three bullet holes in the door above me. So there goes my security deposit.

Maybe the danger has passed. Maybe not. I crawl toward the bedroom where curtains still obscure the only window to be on the safe side. I feel like I'm having a little trouble processing this. Someone is trying to kill me now? Like, for real?

I grab the wheat grass on my way, and when I get to my destination, I present it to Mardy whom seems unfazed by the gunfire. He cocks his head to the side and closes his eyes while he chews the grass. Looks pretty happy to me.

You know what? Killing me in the dream world is one thing, but killing me in real life?

Dick move.

So much for being safe at home.

As the shock fades a bit, I come to a conclusion: When someone tries to kill you, it feels unpleasant. See, there are these emotions inside of me right now that feel all bad and stuff. I don't know. I'm not that great at describing it. Maybe I should have gone to college.

I watch the cat nibble at blades of grass, running back through the event in my mind over and over again. I have a decent sense of "how" this attempt on my life happened, but the "who" and "why" are totally up for grabs. I also still ask myself "what" pretty frequently regarding this matter, as in: What the eff?

Mardy tires of the plant and jumps to find a resting spot at the foot of the bed, folding his feet underneath his body, so that from the back he looks like a loaf of bread with cat fur stretched over it. I consider going back to bed myself but not seriously. I doubt I'd actually sleep at all.

A fragment of Babinaux's warning in the back of the Lincoln flashes in my head. What did she say, again? I could be in danger. They know about my seizures. Many people are invested in my endeavors, some for less than savory reasons.

I guess it's the only thing that makes sense. Someone is trying to kill me because of my dreams.

Tremendous. These seizures are a gift on so many levels.

I reposition myself, still sitting on the floor to avoid getting assassinated via the window. Upon moving, a tingle spreads across my leg, taint and left nard. Much of my lower body has fallen asleep due to my odd floor seating session. The tingle swells into a widespread prickling that creeps and throbs. The nard area proves to be particularly troublesome.

I cry out and move in slow motion to allow relief to happen

while not jostling it into any strong needle prick type feelings. Still, the feeling lingers longer than what seems reasonable before it finally starts to fade out.

Back to my imminent death, though, what options do I really have? I could wait around for someone to try to kill me again. No real upside to going that route, though it's the path of least resistance, the choice I usually opt for. Or I could work with Glenn who has a similar goal and at least some prior connections with these people.

I guess I shouldn't have said "options" after all. I have one option, which makes it more mandatory.

I start looking around at what I'll need to bring with. It won't be safe here for Mardy either, so he'll have to come along. Before I pack everything up, I scrawl a note and magnet it to my fridge:

"Dudes,

Please stop trying to kill me as soon as possible.

Thank you,

Jeff Grobnagger"

- 5 -

Glenn's front door stands before me, a hulking red thing a man and a half wide that makes me feel small. I've already tried the doorbell a few times to no avail, so now the knocking shall commence. My fist pounds the steel, hesitates, bangs again with a little more fervor. I wait, but there's no response. This strikes me as weird because Glenn's Explorer sits in the driveway, pink bumper glaring in the sun. He doesn't seem like the type to sleep in, either.

I linger on the doorstep another moment, and I turn to leave. Whatever. Guess I'll have to try again this afternoon.

As I hit the sidewalk six paces later, however, I hear a sound like a muffled bang. I can't be sure, but it seems like it came from inside Glenn's house.

I head back toward the door and start walking around the perimeter of the building. I peer in the windows along the way, but most of them are covered, and I can't see anything going on in the ones that aren't. There's another bang, definitely coming from inside Glenn's.

Great.

My first thought is that maybe the same person that just tried to shoot me is now going after Glenn. I don't know how much sense that would make, but none of this makes much sense to begin with. The noise doesn't sound like a gunshot,

41

though. It sounds more like something heavy falling or getting bashed against something.

Another crack erupts and is quickly followed by the sound of a man grunting. The voice has that same gritty texture to it that Glenn's had at the u-scan.

I'm scrambling now, moving into the back yard. The smell of cut grass is everywhere. He must have mowed this morning. I twist the knob to the door leading into the garage. It's locked.

I check the windows along the back of the house, but they're all locked, too. I peel around the corner to find a bathroom window cracked. My fingers latch onto the edges of the screen and rip it away from the frame. I throw open the window and climb in.

How ridiculous is this? Yesterday I would've sworn I'd never be back here, and I'm not only back a mere 12 hours later, I'm actually breaking into the place. I guess the complexion of a situation can change once snipers try to shoot you in the face. I think I saw that inspirational message on a mug once.

The walls in the bathroom are sea foam green, and the toilet matches. What a cute place to take a shit, right? I creep to the doorway and poke my head out to look down the hall.

Nothing.

I slip through the doorway and realize a few steps later that I'm doing a weird exaggerated tiptoe walk with my shoulders all hunched over like Nosferatu. I stop doing that and walk in a more normal fashion, though still on the lighter of foot side.

I reach a corner and stop to listen. Though I was just here yesterday, I don't have a great feel for the layout of the house. I can hear a man's voice. It's definitely not Glenn, but it's too quiet to make out any words. The voice sounds oddly upbeat considering the presumed circumstances. Energetic.

I move into the next room – a dining room worthy of a center fold in one of those magazines that interior designers masturbate to. High back chairs upholstered in cream colored velvet surround a table with a top that appears to be one enormous slice of a tree. The surface is polished to a high sheen so it reflects the crystal chandelier overhead almost like a mirror.

As I move past the dining table, I realize that there's music playing. It's fairly soft, but I can make out a pulsing dance music beat. Now things really don't make sense… unless this music is being used as a form of psychological torture, which I've always felt dance music was well suited for. Either way, the music and talking are coming from a door just ahead.

I stand in the hall and watch through the doorway as Glenn bounces around in a small room with an exercise bike and elliptical machine wedged into it. He dances to the right and throws a jab and dances to the left and throws a jab, mirroring the people on his TV including the man with the upbeat voice.

"Uh… hey," I say.

Glenn moves to the heavy bag in the corner, busting into a flurry of squat and punch reps. The bag thuds with each hit, the final punch slamming it into the wall with a reverberating slap that I imagine sounds more like a crack or bang from outside the house.

"Hey!" I say much louder.

He twirls, lays eyes on me, and his brow crinkles. He pops out an earbud.

"How'd you get in here?" he says.

"I rang the bell, but I heard noises, and I thought maybe…"

I trail off, and his confused expression slowly morphs into a smile and a nod.

"Oh, I get it," he says. "You thought I was… That's flippin' hilarious, man. Nah. I'm just doing some Tae Bo."

"I see that."

I didn't know that men do Tae Bo, but I decide not to mention this to Glenn.

I sit in the living room. The house is quiet. Empty. Glenn freaked out about the complete lack of Oreos on hand, pieced together a short grocery list and ran to the store. He didn't ask if I wanted to go, which was perfect because I did not.

Mardy sits on the couch next to me. The two of us watch Leroy peek his head into the room, lock eyes with my cat and then slowly back away. It's weird. So far Glenn's cats are terrified of Mardy. I thought there'd be more feline friction - a blur of claws and fur and guttural sounds - but so far it's just been a couple of hisses and a lot of submission from Leroy and friends. I probably shouldn't be, but I'm kind of proud. My cat is a bad ass.

Before he rushed off, Glenn offered to clear boxes of junk out of the guest room for me to sleep in while I try to avoid getting killed, but I insisted I'd be fine with a sheet and blanket on the sofa. Getting my own room would freak me out somehow. It'd feel too permanent.

I am motionless, sunk into the couch, arms limp at my sides. After 15 minutes of watching dust motes flit around in the bars of sunlight coming through the windows, I finally stir. I head into the kitchen looking for something to drink. I figure

he told me to make myself at home, so I may as well indulge.
Glenn strikes me as the type of man to always keep an
assortment of beverages on hand, and I'm a fan of tasty drinks.

A scent wafts around the kitchen, hops and barley. I spot
two empty Sam Adams bottles in the sink that seem to be the
culprit. I guess Glenn drank a couple of beers after mowing the
lawn earlier.

The smell of pretty much any alcoholic beverage reminds
me of Allie. When we first started hanging out, we drank a lot.
A lot. It was more like nightly races to see who would vomit
first.

I remember how hard she laughed when we were walking
home from a party and I threw up in someone's front yard on
Broad Street and immediately fell in it. And I remember after I
moved in with her, whenever we laid in bed together she always
said my breath smelled like oranges when I drank.

I bring my hand to my brow, a little light headed. The
memories lurch and sway in my brain like if the synapses fire
just right, the people and places from the past can become real
again, take physical shape in Glenn's kitchen, instead of just
being images encoded in the cells in some guy's head.

I sit down at the snack bar to wait for the dizzy spell to pass.
The stench hangs in the air all around me now.

But a smell never conjures just memories of events. It
dredges up all the feelings of that time, all the hopes and
dreams I had when I was young that withered away some time
ago, all the doors long closed, and the way that what seems
possible slowly shifts into something smaller and smaller as
time passes.

I remember lying in bed with Allie, awake in the dark,

listening to her talk about love like it was a magical place we could go together. And I know I believed it at the time. I really did.

But we didn't go there, and I don't believe it anymore.

So yeah, the odor makes me think of Allie, and I don't want to think about her right now.

I rinse out the bottles and toss them in the recycling bin.

- 6 -

Glenn leans over the snack bar with a towel slung over his shoulders. His hair is still wet from the shower. I've filled him in on all the details – the gunfire, the busted door, my most recent trip to Chokington Abbey, the meeting with Ms. Babinaux.

"The way I see it, we've got five mysteries of varying importance laid out in front of us," he says. "Where is my daughter? What's going on in your seizure dreams? What's the deal with the book and sphere from Amity's room? How and what do the cult people know about you? And who is trying to kill you?"

I'm wolfing down another serving of cold chicken, also known as the perfect second breakfast, but I come up for air long enough to chime in.

"That sums it up, though you may have buried the lead a little bit," I say.

Glenn smirks.

"The order we put them in doesn't matter," he says. "Not really, anyhow. They're all intertwined."

"You could be right about that, but I suspect I will be less concerned about solving the other quandaries if I'm deceased," I say.

"We've got to talk to these cult people," he says.

"Might that not be safe?" I say. "I mean, it's the only avenue of investigation I see as well, but if one of them is trying to kill me, I may be better served to keep my distance."

"True," he says. "But Babinaux met with you and warned you, right? She could have just as easily tried to kill you or abduct you at that point, couldn't she?"

"I guess," I say. "Well, you asked around about these cults. Did you hear anything about her?"

"Not much," he says. "Her name came up once that I remember. I got the impression that she's an important player with the League of Light. Perhaps we should start with them."

"Perhaps," I say. "So what are they all about? I take it they are fans of light."

"I'll tell you in the car," he says.

We sit in the Explorer outside of Bucky's Diner, a spot where a bunch of these weirdos hang out according to Glenn. Our mission is to observe from a distance, though I'm not sure how incognito we are with that damn pink bumper gleaming the way it does.

The sign for the diner has a marquee on it, with the letters that can be rearranged to spell out the specials or whatever. The letters read CHOCOLATE CHIP PANCAKES $5.45. One of the 5's is actually an "S". I wonder what goes best on a stack of chocolate chip pancakes. Maple syrup? Seems like overkill. Maybe whipped cream. That sounds pretty tasty.

After a few minutes I'm bored with thinking about pancakes and their hypothetical toppings.

"What exactly are we even looking for?" I say. "So far I've gleaned that the people in the diner drink a lot of coffee."

"We've been here for about three minutes, buddy. Have you ever thought about how impatient you are?" Glenn says. "You know that's going to get you in trouble one of these days."

"Whatever," I say.

"The three guys in the corner booth are in the League," he says. "And the man and woman seated at the counter are as well. I'm sure there are others."

I look them over.

"How can you even tell?" I say.

"I recognize two of the guys in the booth from my prior poking around. They struck me as amateurs," he says. "And the guy and girl each have the sigil on their backpacks."

"Oh," I say. "Right."

We fall silent. I watch the waitress tote two carafes of coffee around to give refills, but my mind starts to wander again. My eyes trace up and down the cracks in the brick façade. The building falls just short of what I would call crumbling, but it's getting there.

"Why do they hang out at this diner?" I say. "Seems like a dump."

"The owner is sympathetic to the cause," he says. "Plus the coffee has caffeine in it, and the burgers ain't bad."

"OK, so they're here, and they're eating," I say. "Now what?"

"Now we exercise patience," he says.

I wait and watch, and the minutes drag by. People stab at pieces of pie with their forks and shovel various soups into their faces. They guzzle colas. They gobble French fries. They generally gorge themselves. It's all quite boring.

"Are we going to go in?" I say.

"Not yet," he says.

"What are we waiting for?" I say.

"An opening," he says.

I think about pointing out that the door is just the opening we need to get in there, but I decide against it. Glenn seems to know what he's doing, or at least he thinks he does. I can go with it.

"So weren't you going to tell me about the League and all of that?" I say.

"Huh?" Glenn says, his eyes still fastened to the dining weirdos. "Oh, right. Yeah."

He wiggles in his seat for a second, I think to adjust the angle of his lower back.

"The League of Light started all of this," he says. "They're into your pretty basic occult stuff – Qabalah, Tarot, various forms of unorthodox spiritual development. Eventually a sect splintered off, calling themselves the Disunion of Shadows."

"Disunion?" I say.

He nods.

"The Disunion's premise is that all modern religions, including the League, worship order too much," he says. "They believe that chaos comprises the other half of human nature – sort of a left brain and right brain thing, I guess. In the end, it's a lot of the same stuff – Qabalah, Tarot and so on – but the Disunion people pursue all of it in the interest of finding a balance between chaos and order. An organization based on Chaos is sort of an oxymoron, right? That's why they named it the Disunion."

"I see," I say. "That's kind of interesting, I guess. I just assumed these people were all dumbasses that burn black candles and pretend weird stuff."

Glenn glances at me.

"I've read a couple of the books and all the articles I could find," he says. "Some of it makes you think. Other stuff is about whacking off while focusing on a particular Tarot card."

I laugh.

"See?" I say. "That's more like what I was imagining."

Inside the diner, the patrons seem to be gathering around a man with a shaved head clad in black. He stands at a table in the center of the room.

"This is it," Glenn says, digging around under the seat.

He pulls an unidentifiable piece of flattened blue fabric from the floor and massages it back into the shape of a baseball cap. It's the trucker style with the mesh in the back, and it says in black letters, "My Wife is on The Warpath again."

"Put this on," he says.

"Not a chance," I say.

He huffs.

"Just do it," he says. "We're running out of time."

I look at the hat again for a moment before I take it from him and slide it on. He finds and pulls on his own, which is covered in fake bird poop and says "DAMN SEAGULLS," in all caps. I'm not sure why he feels like that's a better disguise than his normal blue hat, but he does. At least I'm not the only one wearing a hat with a dumb slogan on it.

"Did you have to throw darts at balloons at the county fair to win these?" I say.

His eyes are fixed on the diner, though, and he doesn't respond for a second.

"What?" he says.

"Nothing," I say.

"OK, listen," he says. "Keep your head down. Don't make eye contact. Don't say anything. I'll do the talking. Let's go."

We leave the Explorer and file into the restaurant. The hat makes me a little self conscious, but nobody looks our way when we walk in. All eyes focus on the man in black.

"Here," Glenn whispers, gesturing to a booth in the corner.

We sit. Glenn turns his coffee cup over, and a waitress fills it within seconds. I order some fries and a coke.

Across the diner to my right, a man and a woman hold hands on the table top in their booth. She has dark hair and eyes that perpetually look like she is about to start laughing. He is bald with a beard that's a bit too well kept. Fussy. He looks too serious.

Right away, I think she could do better.

I look over my shoulder to see what the man in black is up to. He clenches a spoon in his fist with his arm fully extended in front of his body. His nose wrinkles as he squints at the spoon, and the crowd watches this, rapt, like he's holding a grenade or maybe a baby elephant instead of a spoon. He's really putting some stank on it, too. His knuckles are all white.

I open my mouth to say "Pretty cool spoon," but Glenn must know I'm about to do this, so he kicks my shin under the table. I gasp in pain, and Glenn shout whispers:

"Stop it!"

Now, this is annoying on a couple of levels. First of all, he's not my grandma, and we're not at church. I'm pretty sure both of those conditions must be met to legally justify the use of the shout whisper. Second of all, his stupid whisper is louder than my gasp, thereby more than defeating the purpose in this scenario. Nobody notices either of them, anyway, so it's a moot point.

I look at Glenn, half tempted to test him a bit out of annoyance, but his face looks a little redder than usual and his mustache is twitching like a squirrel's mouth, both of which I take as signs of grave seriousness. He shakes his head at me, and his cheeks jiggle, however, undermining said seriousness.

I look back at the man in black, and he's slowly uncurling his fingers from the spoon. His face looks all sweaty and flushed, and he's panting not unlike a German Shepherd. His fingers peel back one by one and pretty soon he's not holding the spoon at all, it's just kind of stuck to his palm. And I'm thinking, "Big deal, this guy stuck a spoon to his palm."

Then he pulls his whole hand back, but the spoon stays there, hovering in the air before him. Floating. Levitating. I don't even know why I know the word levitating, but I am witnessing that shit right now.

The crowd gasps. A little kid with curly red hair in the booth in front of ours brings a hand up to cover his gaping mouth, and then I realize that I just did the same thing.

The man in black moves his hand in a circular motion a few times about two feet from the spoon, until the spoon seems to catch on to the motion like a magnet suddenly pulling something close. It's not drawn to his hand, though, it's drawn to the motion and traces it in the air. He hesitates a moment, and then winds up and pushes the spoon without touching it in one violent heave like someone throwing a shot put. The spoon angles up and up, flying across the room and slamming against the spot where the ceiling meets the wall on the opposite side of the diner before clanging to the floor.

The crowd erupts in applause, and we all stand up simultaneously. Goose bumps crawl down the lengths of my arms. Weird feelings swell in my gut like I've just witnessed something special. Almost like a miracle. Part of my brain is asking whether or not that could be real, and the rest of my brain is screaming, "Yes, it's real! Are you kidding, shithead? I just saw it with our own two eyes!"

I can't stop tracing the spoon's flight path with my gaze. The straight line that leads from the hand of the man in black to the wall across the room. It's a good 20 feet or so. Spoon marks pock up and down the wall, and I realize this has happened many times before. It's a routine.

I glance at Glenn, and he's clapping, but he looks a little indifferent.

Wait a minute.

Am I a dumbass that just got duped? It looked real and all, but Glenn seems like the type that would be eating this up. I mean, he was impressed by my cavalier attitude toward the manager at Meijer, which pales in comparison to this robust display of telekinesis. I would have thought he'd at least be dabbing tears of wonder out of his eyes with a Kleenex at this point if not openly weeping.

I turn back just as the man in black stands upright again, and a hush comes over the crowd. He stretches his arms out to the sides, crucifixion-style, and closes his eyes. He stands that way for a long moment, arms open wide.

I scan the faces in the crowd. Everyone that I can see looks like they're experiencing something religious except for Glenn and a girl in a lime green shirt across the room. She even meets my eyes and smiles as I glance at her. This kind of freaks me out, so I look away really fast.

I remember that I'm wearing the hat. Maybe she was smiling because she thinks my wife really is on the warpath.

Veins begin to bulge in the man in black's neck, and his shoulders quiver. His face reddens and slowly darkens toward purple. As spit hisses between his teeth, the lights in the room shut off for a fraction of a second and flip back on. Several people in the crowd moan. I crane my neck to check the lights for a second, and when I look back, the man in black is flickering. There's an electrical buzz as he flickers between what looks like a solid version of himself and a faded, translucent version of himself. A few sparks start flying from the floor beneath him.

I expect him to let up any second, but he hunches down, his whole body quivering now as he looks to dig in and push even harder. The pace of the flicker picks up, closing in on strobe light levels. His lips curl back now, baring clenched teeth. The skin on his face is the color of a yellowed page in an old paperback book.

"Stop," a voice nearby says.

"Stop it!" a lady toward the front yells.

Additional voices rise in a cacophony more or less urging him to quit, some seemingly saying it more to themselves, some screaming at the man, pleading with him.

The buzzing sound builds to a roar. The man looks like he's gone limp, like the electric current in the air around him is the only thing holding him up.

And then he disappears. He's just gone.

The buzzing stops, and the room falls to silence. Nobody moves.

And the lights turn off again. People stir, and the volume cranks back up on the tangled web of voices.

The light comes back on, and the man in black is back, arms crossed over his heaving chest. He smiles, and everyone bursts into applause again, even rowdier than the last time. You can feel all the tension in the room turn into relief and adoration.

He doesn't sit down so much as free fall into his chair with a plop. It gets a huge laugh.

The applause finally starts to die down, and the normal diner sounds start to return as people sit – clinking coffee cups, forks scraping plates, a bus boy dumping piles of dishes in the sink. I remain standing longer than most, though.

"OK," I say. "THAT was fucking awesome."

I realize right after I say this that I'm talking too loud. I guess I wasn't saying it to Glenn so much as addressing the room at large. For a moment, I feel like we were all together in witnessing something awesome, but I know the universe will make me pay for expressing this feeling.

A bunch of heads snap around to look at me. The girl in the lime green shirt laughs really hard. She tries to stifle it by literally biting her fist. The man in black stands up, and I realize that he's also staring at me. He claps twice.

"Uh, sorry," I say.

I sit down. There's a moment of hesitation, and then the man in black turns and walks out the door with about two thirds of the rest of the diners following him. Most technically stand in line to pay their bill rather than walking straight out, but as I look around I see a lot of half eaten meals, abandoned at the behest of two claps from the leader.

Well, this is embarrassing. I feel warmth crawl across my face, settling on my cheeks. I'm guessing they're about as pink as Glenn's bumper just now.

I don't look at Glenn. My plan, at this juncture, is to just never look at Glenn again. I figure this way I should be fine.

I stare at the wall as Glenn sighs heavily three times. The first time sounds angry. I almost want to look to see if his mustache is doing that squirrel twitch again, but I worry that if I lock eyes with him he'll have an Incredible Hulk type reaction and smash me and everything else in the diner.

His second sigh sounds more frustrated than angry. I guess maybe it's like the stages of death. Acceptance slowly creeps in there.

The third sigh sounds bewildered, like when a dog realizes you're not going to give him any of the pizza you're eating.

Glenn rises from the booth and grunts at me. The sound goes up at the end like it's a question. I take it to mean, "Ready to go?"

"Mmhm," I grunt back.

We pay the bill and exit the diner.

We came. We saw. We did not conquer.

- 7 -

We sit in the Explorer outside the diner for a bit, regrouping. Glenn keeps his hands on the wheel in a way that seems a little aggressive, and I can see muscles bulging at his temples and along his jaw.

"How did they know who I was?" I say.

He shrugs.

"Hard to say," he says. "Perhaps if you'd have kept your mouth shut as I specifically requested…"

He trails off.

"It probably wouldn't have mattered," he says. "I could see it in their faces. They knew who you were right away. We never would have gotten anyone to talk to us."

I shudder at the thought of all of these people talking about me and knowing who I am. I mean, I literally shudder, my torso flailing in an involuntary manner. Somehow Glenn fails to notice this.

"So who was the man in black?" I say.

"Riston Farber," he says. "One of the League hot shots."

"You didn't seem that impressed with his performance," I say.

"I wasn't," he says.

I thought back to the flight of the spoon and Farber flickering out of existence. I'm not sure if I could have been more impressed. Seriously, even if it was sheer trickery, I would pay money to watch that again. Glenn's expression looks sour enough that I decide not to press him on this one, though.

"So what do we do now?" I say.

Glenn huffs through his nose, a snort of laughter that comes across as bitter as aspirin.

"You tell me," he says.

"Maybe there's some way we can contact Babinaux," I say. "If not, she said she'd be in touch soon."

The creases etched into his face soften ever so faintly.

"True," he says. "Maybe waiting is all we can do for now."

Just then there's a knock at my window. It startles me, and I jump straight up, high enough to bang my head on the ceiling. For a split second all I can think is that I'm going to die here, picturing my blood pooling on the leather seats.

I turn, and it's the girl in the lime green shirt. She's laughing again. I guess because of the way I jumped. She makes me uncomfortable. I want to warn Glenn about her, but he's already putting down the window.

"You guys want to talk?" she says.

"Get in," Glenn says.

He presses the power lock button, a series of loud clicks and clacks ensue, and she climbs into the backseat.

"We shouldn't stay around here. Drive," she says.

We do.

I don't like her being behind me, because she can see me and I can't see her. On the other hand, it'd be too overwhelming – too confrontational - to look back. She's just back there in the growing shadows of dusk. I have to will myself to not shudder again.

"I'm Louise," she says. "Louise Lockhart."

"Name's Glenn Floyd," he says, offering a hand over his shoulder which she shakes.

"I'm Jeff Grobnagger," I say.

I have to turn back. It's like getting sucked into a tractor beam because once you face her, you can't turn away. I'm too nervous to shake her hand, so I give a little wave. She smiles at me, and right away I notice that I like her teeth.

"Oh, trust me, I've heard all about the great and powerful Jeffrey Grobnagger," she says. "After that hilarity in there, I had to see you up close for myself."

I swallow, which somehow is super loud. This sets her off laughing again.

The sky around us dims to purple. The half light softens the edges of everything in the car except for Louise's face. Her creamy complexion glows, the dark making it look an almost lilac shade.

"So you know who he is, and you're still talking to us?" Glenn says.

"Yep," she says.

"Aren't there orders or something to not talk to us?" he says.

"There are, but I'm not one of those wackos. I just play one as part of my day job," she says.

"And what is your day job?" he says.

"I'm a private investigator," she says. "I'd ask you guys to keep that to yourselves, but none of the people that matter will even talk to you, so what's the difference, I figure."

"So someone is paying you to keep an eye on the League," he says.

"That's right," she says. "Of course I wouldn't divulge my client's name, but in this case I don't even know who the client is. Some rich guy wants to anonymously overpay me to watch some wackos perform parlor tricks at a diner and suck down cheap coffee at unbearably dull meetings? No sweat off my cheeks."

"So you think they were parlor tricks?" I say.

I am somehow not shocked when she laughs.

"Farber sells it really well. I'll give him that. I'm sorry to be the one to tell you this, Jeffrey, but there's no such thing as real magic," she says. "If you saw Criss Angel mind freaking at that diner, you'd probably stain your shorts brown."

Glenn lets out a weird clucking laugh, apparently finding all of this amusing. Maybe I'm biased, but I think Glenn was a lot cooler when he thought I was awesome and wasn't laughing when people picked on me.

The Explorer meanders through an industrial neighborhood, taking lefts and rights at whims. As we get farther and farther out of town, more of the factories sport overgrown lawns. The rows of windows still smile as wide as ever, but some of the teeth are busted out.

"So what do you want from us?" he says.

"What do you mean?" she says.

"I mean, you approached us. You want to talk to us," he says. "Must be something in it for you."

"That's fair," she says. "I'm curious to know about Jeffrey's dreams. I've heard a lot of rumors."

"Then maybe we can trade," he says.

"Sure," she says.

I decide to take the reins.

61

"How do they know about me and my dreams?" I say.

"That's a good question," she says. "I don't know, to be honest with you. I get the sense that all they really know is that you're having these dreams. I don't think they know much about the actual contents of your dreams or anything like that. It's sort of like they can check the box score in the paper, but that's not the same thing as watching the game, you know what I mean?"

"Wouldn't that suggest that they can do more than parlor tricks, though?" I say. "I mean, if they can somehow check the box scores, like you said, and know who is having these kinds of dreams, it has to mean something, doesn't it?"

"Not necessarily," she says. "Haven't you had at least one of these episodes in public?"

"Well, yeah," I say.

"These freaks get around, and word about this kind of crap gets around even faster," she says. "Believe me, they'd claim to somehow have that ability whether they had it or not."

"So are they trying to kill me?" I say.

"No," she says. "They think you're really important. They're all stressed out about not wanting to 'tamper' with you. That's the word they always use. 'Tamper.'"

"See?" I say. "I can respect that. Why doesn't everyone stop tampering with me already?"

"What about the Disunion?" Glenn says. "Could they be the ones that tried to kill Grobnagger?"

"I doubt it," she says. "The whole chaos thing makes them sound scary, but I've spent some time with them, too. Their version of chaos is more like 'Let's do bong rips, eat nachos and sleep on the beach.'"

"So they're hippies?" I say.

"Pretty much," she says.

"This information isn't turning out to be that useful," I say.

Glenn scratches his chin.

"I'm just answering your questions," she says. "You don't like it, ask better ones."

We fall silent. The Explorer juts left on a dirt road. We're well out of town now, so woods line the roadsides. All I can see in the dark is a thick mess of trees and brush that make me uneasy. Gravel flies up and clinks against the undercarriage in a way that somehow accentuates the quiet in the Explorer. Finally, Louise speaks:

"Here's something. They don't talk about it at their general meetings or anything, but I've overheard some of the League higher ups talking about another group. They call themselves 'The Sons of Man,'" she says. "I guess some members of both the League and the Disunion are rumored to secretly comprise this underground group. They're supposed to be the biggest psychos out of all these people. They want to make man divine. While the others want to understand divinity, these guys want to use stuff like your dreams to become all powerful themselves. Sounds pretty ridiculous to me, but I know the League people are scared shitless of this prospect."

"Doesn't seem like killing me would help them achieve their goal," I say.

"Well, nothing will actually help them achieve their goal," she says. "They're lunatics. Who knows what they might be thinking? Maybe they think they need to sacrifice the great and powerful Jeffrey to get what they want, right?"

"I guess," I say.

"Anyway, I can't read their minds, but I happen to think that was some useful info nonetheless, so let's hear about those dreams already," she says.

I look at Glenn, and he nods, so I tell her about the dreams. She laughs frequently, so I start playing up the absurdities and funny qualities. At least we can agree that some of the things that happen as I get killed over and over again are pretty hilarious. I consider holding back some details here and there, but I think the fact that she doesn't even believe in any of this makes that seem pretty pointless. I tell it all.

While I'm talking, we make our way back into the city. It's not long before we're back, and we drop Louise near the diner.

"I'll keep my eyes and ears open regarding those trying to end your life," she says. "In fact, I must demand that you don't die anytime too soon."

"Why is that?" I say.

"Well, there's a new Thai restaurant on Forbes Street, and I'm going to need you to take me there on Saturday," she says. "I assume you'll be at Glenn's. I'll pick you up around 7."

I don't know what to say, so I say nothing.

"See you soon, Grobnagger," she says.

She turns and walks away.

"Nice," Glenn says.

He bashes a semi-closed hand into my shoulder like he's a football coach and I just came up with a fumble recovery.

"I don't know how you pulled that one off," he says. "But I'll tell you what, she's got a tight little body on her."

"Shut up," I say.

To my surprise, I sound pretty defensive about this. I can't decide if I'm offended that he said that about Louise in particular, or if I'm just generally grossed out by this old guy saying sexually charged shit to me.

"What?" he says. "I'm a man. I notice a nice looking lady when I see one. Is that a crime all of the sudden?"

"Well, notice all you want with your goddamn mouth shut," I say.

Glenn snorts in a way that straddles the line between laughter and disgust. It's the kind of sound a particularly arrogant horse would make, I think.

- 8 -

My consciousness fades in all flicker-y like I can feel the electrical charge coursing through my brain. Like I can see it distorting my vision for a moment before the gray all around me comes into focus. I sigh and reach up to start working the knot out of the rope.

You know what? This alley is the goddamn worst.

But I know what I'm going to do this time. No hiding in the dumpster. No climbing any walls. I'm keeping it real simple this time around.

My feet hit the ground, and I sway for a moment but keep my balance. Here's where my big plan comes into play: I stand. I don't run. I don't walk. I stand. I wipe non-existent dust off of my shirt out of some post fall habit. Other than that? Standing, mostly.

I hear footsteps, and the hooded man hustles around the corner into the alley.

"Hi," I say.

He keeps rushing toward me without a word. Not a big talker, I guess, more of the strong, silent type.

"My name is Jeff," I say. "Jeff Grobnagger. I don't know why I'm here. I don't know why you're here. All I know is that some people are trying to kill me in real life, and my friend Glenn's daughter is missing. Amity. I think it all has something to do with me coming here."

The man slows, still moving toward me but with hesitation. This is good.

"Do you know where we are?" I say.

No response. He keeps walking toward me, but he's just barely creeping at this point. I realize for the first time that he's not nearly as big as I always thought. He might even be slightly smaller than me. I guess your perspective changes when people hover over you for a good strangle. They suddenly seem quite substantial.

"Can't we just talk about this?" I say. "Can you communicate with me, or is that forbidden or something?"

He shrugs. This is new.

I start pivoting away from him like a defensive boxer circling the perimeter of the ring to keep the slugger out of knockout range. He seems content to let me stay just out of reach, though he never stops pursuing me completely. He shrugged, remember? We're practically best friends now.

"Holy shit!" I say. "Are you bleeding?"

I point at his belly and turn to run in one motion. As I suspect, he is thrown by all of this and looks at his belly for a moment as I pull away from him. I look back over my shoulder to see his gaze turn away from his stomach. He begins to give chase. This is by far the best lead I've had on him to date.

I fly. My feet have an extra bounce when they come off of the ground. I tell myself I'm the fastest man in all of the damn dream world, and it feels like it. My feet are so light, like if I concentrated hard enough I could burst into the air and never come back down.

No running around the block this time. I move away from

the alley in as straight of a line as I can, though the street I'm on has some curves to it. Straight-ish, in any case.

I glance over my shoulder just in time to see him stumble over a curb. How humiliating. He's so far back there. He looks tinier than ever. The only thing getting strangled today is this poor bastard's pride.

I get to a fork in the road. Both sides look pretty much identical. If I had to describe them, I'd say that they're gray. The buildings are pretty nondescript. The air seems to move, like smoke or something, in the distance. I veer left. I don't know why, really. Left seems cooler.

Another over the shoulder glance reveals the hooded man to have fallen even farther back. Embarrassing. The part of me that could have become a gym teacher wants to yell at him to quit lollygaggin' and/or playing grab-ass back there. The rest of me stays focused on the running thing.

This doesn't seem like him. He's usually an efficient killing machine. Did my talking to him throw him this far off of his game?

I bank around a curve and begin mounting a steep hill. It strikes me that I'm not out of breath. My legs don't feel tired at all. It's almost like all of me knows this isn't all the way real or something, and I don't have to get tired here anymore.

As I summit the top of the hill, I see a wall of fog about a half of a block in front of me. Thick fog. It doesn't look right. It starts too abruptly, and I can see nothing through it. Just dark gray, almost black. The fog wall stretches as far as I can see in both directions. I realize that it likely forms a perimeter around the entire area. It surrounds us.

I reach the fog and stop. It makes me uncomfortable to be

this close to it. I stick my hand in, and it's like it disappears. It's so cold. I pull my fist back, and for a second my fingers look all gray before the color comes back to them.

Great.

I picture myself taking a step into the fog and freefalling out into nothing. That's all I can imagine: nothing on the other side. Not dark. Not blackness. An absence of anything. It seems like that could be worse than getting strangled.

I sit down on the asphalt. I could run, but apparently there's nowhere to go.

The man arrives soon, and he makes quick work of things.

He's good at his job. I can respect that.

I wake up in the Explorer with Glenn staring at me. I look around and see the headlights catching on the rose bushes on either side of the big red door. We're in Glenn's driveway.

"Another seizure, huh?" he says.

"Yes," I say.

The events flash through my head. When I remember that fog it makes me feel sad in a way that doesn't really make sense. Like I've lost something. I don't remember things going black this time, which bothers me. I know the seizures are happening more frequently. Maybe they are coming on quicker, too.

"I figured," he says. "You fished out again. Flopped around like a pair of boobs on a treadmill. Got a real sick look about you toward the end there, too. I thought you were going to upchuck on the leather."

He taps and then pets the head rest like it's something precious.

"Yeah, I'm fine," I say. "Thanks for asking."

"Uh… sorry," he says. "Look, this Explorer is my baby. Eddie Bauer edition. I get carried away about taking care of her sometimes."

"It's ok," I say.

I suppress the urge to mention that this is an '02 with a flaming pink bumper.

"Any new developments?" he says. "In your dream?"

"Yeah," I say. "I got to the edge of the world, I think."

"Oh?" he says. "What was that like?"

"Foggy," I say. "It's a wall of fog that drops off into nothing."

He taps on the steering wheel as he mulls this over.

"Well, at least you know that running away isn't the solution to the test," he says.

"I guess."

"We should get some sleep," he says, opening the door. "Tomorrow is a new day. New days bring new ideas."

- 9 -

I sit on the couch in Glenn's living room, twisting and jabbing at the puzzle sphere in my hands. No progress, though. I've tried googling a few of the hieroglyphic like symbols, but I didn't find much of interest. They're not from the ancient Egyptian hieroglyphic alphabet as it happens. I guess that's important to know. It does not get me any closer to opening the damn thing, however.

Knowing my luck, after hours of painstaking research I will figure this thing out only to learn that once you unlock it, you're whisked away to another dimension where a hooded man strangles you to death in an alley. Hardy har har.

After a few more random and failed attempts at popping the sphere open, I nestle it down into the cushions of the couch so it doesn't roll away, and I reach for my Arnold Palmer on the end table. The glass moistens my fingers with condensation, and the ice cubes tinkle within. I take a long drink. Half lemonade + half iced tea = one full awesome. Pretty sure Glenn is some kind of food wizard. Everything he touches turns to delish.

He retired for the evening a little while ago, but I'm not tired yet. It must be weird to get old. Does every day tire you out? I guess I can see how that shift has already started for me. It wasn't long ago that I would stay up until 4 or 5 am watching movies and such. There would be no real ill effects the next day. If I try to pull something like that now, the next day is miserable.

As I set the sweaty glass back down, movement catches the corner of my eye. I turn my head to see lights flickering on and off out the window. Headlights. It's too dark to be sure, but it looks like a dark colored Lincoln. I think I know what this is about.

I gather myself, slide my feet into my shoes, take one more drink of tea-monade and head for the door. As my hand nears the knob, I pause for a moment. I turn back and grab the sphere, lodging it into my hoodie pocket. It bulges, stretching the fabric like my sweatshirt has a small pregnant belly.

As I get outside, a man in a suit stands outside the car. He opens his mouth to speak, but I interrupt:

"Babinaux?" I say.

"Yes," he says, but I'm in the backseat before he can even finish the word.

Ms. Babinaux sports a black blouse that I think sort of looks like something a pirate would wear, all puffy and stuff. The collar winds up around her neck.

Our hands clasp, and we say hi.

"It's good to see you in one piece, Mr. Grobnagger," she says. "I heard about what happened to your apartment."

"Where'd you hear that?" I say, settling into my seat.

She pushes her hair behind her ears before she replies.

"You're OK, though?" she says. "You're staying with a friend?"

"Yeah, I'm fine," I say, though I note that she dodged my question entirely. "Any idea who would want me dead?"

She squints.

"It doesn't make much sense to me," she says and shakes her head.

Again, she fails to answer my query, being indirect. I have no idea if this is any way significant, but it makes me uneasy.

"Are you ready to explain anything to me?" I say.

"It's tricky to know what to tell. There are so many moving parts," she says. "Much remains unclear."

"Sure, sure," I say. "Another productive meeting here in the backseat of your car."

Her eyebrows dart up. I don't think she anticipated my sarcasm. She smiles after that, but I don't quite buy it.

"I can explain things in vague terms," she says. "As far as I know, there'd be no reason to hurt you. There may be a group that would want to use you, but the who, how and why of the matter remain mysterious."

"The Sons of Man?" I say.

The eyebrows jerk again.

"Where'd you hear that name?" she says.

"People talk," I say. "I listen."

"Jeffrey, I really need to know who told you about this," she says.

"I can explain it in vague terms," I say, my tone conveying the faintest mocking lilt. "A carbon based life form may have told me about it, but this being remains mysterious."

She squints in a way that is somehow intimidating. It suddenly occurs to me that this lady may be capable of a supernova level of rage, so I quickly change the subject:

"Oh hey," I say, pulling the puzzle sphere from my hoodie pocket. "What can you tell me about this?"

She looks at the sphere, and I think I detect a faint eye roll, but it's subtle to the point that I'm not sure.

"Are you serious?" she says.

"I never joke around about puzzle spheres. Ever. Have you ever seen one like it?" I say.

"I've seen a whole display of them," she says.

Wait. Am I missing something? I speak slowly. I can almost hear my dumb brain trying to work this out.

"A whole display?" I say.

"The answers you seek are at the mall, Mr. Grobnagger," she says.

I don't know what to say. She taps a fingernail on the sphere, each impact tinkling a high pitched metallic sound.

"They sell those at the Sharper Image," she says. "Or at least they did a couple of years ago. Sort of a novelty item."

"Oh," I say.

I take another look at the sphere. I guess the ornate grooves in the maroon casing do seem like something stamped out in a factory mass production style more than they seem like some hand crafted product from long ago. Glenn is going to be disappointed to learn this.

"I bet you could find Youtube videos about how to open it, if that's what you're asking," she says, handing the object back to me.

"Yes," I say. "That makes sense."

I shove the sphere back into my hoodie pocket. I can't bear to look at the damn thing. I feel the warmth crawl up onto my cheeks, and I can only imagine the shade of red they're achieving at the moment. To go from all of my sarcasm and truculence to this Sharper Image reveal somehow makes me feel so dumb that I just want to crawl under a floppy dead dog and die.

The next morning I turn on the water, tweaking the knobs back and forth in the eternal struggle to find a sweet spot between frigid and scalding in someone else's bathroom. Pretty sure this can't be done. Anyway, the water pressure seems pretty intense to me as I pass my hand through the stream to check the temp. This suspicion is confirmed when I step into the shower for real. It stings and leaves pink marks where it hits my body. Not out of heat – it's actually on the lukewarm side – out of sheer liquid force. It's like cleaning yourself with a fire hose on full blast. And I can't help but think that if the water got a direct nut shot, it'd rip my sack clean off.

How the hell does a man live like this? In America? These are third world, sack ripping conditions.

I crank the heat up a bit, and the bathroom fills with steam and the sound of the water slapping the tub. I accent that soundtrack periodically with gasps and whimpers as the water tries its best to remove flesh from bone. I soap and rinse, but more than that, I endure.

Upon stepping out, however, I realize how clean I feel. Like all the strangling just got washed away. Maybe power washed away is the more accurate way to say it. Either way, it feels like all traces of the alley just got blasted off my being and sent spiraling down the drain even if I know that isn't physically true.

I bury my face in the fluff of a towel and then wrap it around my waist and move toward the sink. The tiles underfoot give off shocking warmth. Heated flooring? This luxury stands in glaring contrast to the abomination Glenn is trying to pass off as a shower head.

I wipe a circle of steam off of the mirror with the heel of my hand. Pink swirls blotch the skin on my chest and neck, but I'm still here, and I am awake.

In the kitchen, Glenn pushes a glass of something green over to me. I lift the glass and examine its contents. It's a thick liquid about the shade of grass, completely opaque. It smells a little familiar. Some type of fruit juice, I suppose, but I can't place it.

"What is it?" I say.

"Just try it," he says. "Then I'll tell."

I take a sip. It's interesting. A very fresh flavor. A little sweet, like maybe there's some apple in there, but nowhere near as sweet as your average fruit juice.

"You like?" he says.

"It's pretty good," I say. "So what is it?"

"The green giant," he says. "My own recipe - a bunch of kale, lettuce, carrots, cucumbers, oranges and apples. Tossed into the juicer and stirred, not shaken."

"For real?" I say.

He nods. I take another sip. I guess I can detect the greens if I really think about it, but it's a tasty beverage nonetheless.

"You're basically taking in a huge salad's worth of vitamins and nutrients right now, Grobnagger," he says. "I try to make sure to have a glass four or five times a week."

When I tell Glenn what Ms. Babinaux said about the sphere, he pinches his eyes closed and exhales deeply. His torso sags like a deflating beach ball.

"The Sharper Image?" he says. "Ugh. The worst."

His eyelids part in slow motion. He picks up the sphere from the counter, paws at it, turns it over in his hands.

"Damn," he says, setting it back down. "That's a kick in the sack."

"There could still be something inside of it," I say. "Something important, you know?"

The right side of his mouth curls into a smirk that reminds me of a child that just found out that Santa Claus is a complete fabrication.

"Maybe," he says.

We move to Glenn's computer. A Youtube search reveals several videos regarding how to open the sphere. One guy takes a titanium drill bit to it - pretty entertaining but probably not the route for us to pursue. Other techniques involve a little more precision and nuance. Interestingly, two of the three golden dials are for show and have nothing to do with cracking the puzzle.

After we watch a few videos, Glenn gives it a go. He seems to do the first couple of steps correctly, but something goes wrong, and when he presses the button and tries to pull the top free, the sphere remains locked up tighter than a clam.

He doesn't say anything. He just hands me the puzzle, and I know it's my turn.

First, I spin the middle dial to the left, slowly and with care, until I hear the ball bearing inside descend with a metallic chirp and clank. Next, I spin the dial back to the right, once again all slow and deliberate, until I hear a second chirp and clank as the ball bearing descends another level. This is where a little muscle comes in. I whack the puzzle sphere on the corner of the desk.

In retrospect, I believe this to be where Glenn's attempt went awry. He tried to merely bang it on his palm. I give it a much stiffer thump.

I depress the shiny button on top, and I hear the ball bearing move again, more of a scrape than a chirp this time. Still holding the button, I ease my fingernails into the seam and pull on the top. It's stuck. I can feel the two halves still grabbing hold of each other like a tick shoulders deep in a dog's ear. It's not going to work after all.

I adjust my fingers and try one more hard pull. The metal moans and then pops as the top and bottom disengage, the half closest to me yanking free before the other side. For a moment I pause with the two halves of the globe about an inch apart and still facing each other and make eye contact with the Glenn. His eyes glow, his beach ball abdomen puffed back up into something proud. He nods at me, and I open the sphere.

There's a spring inside the top half, and a metal cylinder with a hole in the bottom. The cylinder must house the ball bearing as it's nowhere to be seen.

The bottom half has a small chamber hollowed out in the center. There's something in it, wrapped in a torn piece of notebook paper.

I set the top half on the desk and hold the bottom half up to Glenn as though serving him an hors d'oeuvre. His mouth is slightly agape as he pulls the object from the shell and unwraps it.

"Another one?" he says, squinting at the item in his hands.

He tilts his palm toward me so I can see. The paper is blank. Inside is a key.

-10-

The airport is the worst. The hordes of travelers open their eyes a little too wide and snap their heads around to watch all the moving parts around them. They huddle around in clusters and talk in semi-hushed tones. They check their phones and watches every two seconds, generally struggling to hold still. It all reminds me of insects.

Anxiety is contagious, I think. Perhaps it's transmittable by sweat and/or body odor.

We weave through crowds of fidgety people toward the lockers. They try to press their nervous smell all up on us. They hover too close and stop in our path. They lean in our direction. If it were socially acceptable to smear their pit stains on our persons, they'd probably never stop doing it.

Glenn has a determined look about him, which I guess makes sense since we stand to finally learn something about Amity. He jostles his way in front of me to take the lead. I don't realize at first that he does so with a clear purpose in mind.

He has a new vision for airport maneuvering. Namely this vision entails jabbing his elbow into the lower back of anyone that crowds in front of him and bellowing:

"LOOK OUT."

If ever words were spoken in all caps, these were those words.

And somehow it works. People clear out of his way like cars pulling over to let an ambulance through. He looks quite pleased with himself. Watching him, I almost wish I was older. I feel like if you're over 50 and do something like this, everyone just complies. You're somehow not to be trifled with.

We arrive at the lockers and scan for G-123, find it, pop in the key and turn that shit. Glenn takes a deep breath and pulls the door open all slow. Like this is a game show, and he's revealing the prize behind Door Number One.

Inside sits one of those black and white composition notebooks. We just stare at it a moment before Glenn scoots it toward us and then lifts it. The notebook fall open in his hands. He flicks through a few pages, but I can't see anything.

"A diary," he says. "Amity's diary."

I sit on Glenn's couch while he reads the diary in the next room. He doesn't insist on us being in separate rooms for this. I do. I figure it best to give him some space. It must be weird to read your daughter's private thoughts, right?

On TV there's a montage of a couple falling in love. The girl sports blindingly white teeth. The guy's jaw displays just the right amount of five o'clock shadow. It's a rapid fire offensive of clichés: They laugh in a movie theater. They get stuck at the top of the Ferris wheel. They hold hands on the beach. They dance all slow. I'm just waiting for them to do the spaghetti thing from "Lady and the Tramp."

I keep realizing that I'm staring at the wall instead of the TV screen. I can barely stand to watch this blossoming romance, I guess, so I keep subconsciously subverting my gaze.

I know this is fictional, but… She could do better, anyway.

For real.

Glenn strides into the room and plops the journal down on the couch next to me. He avoids eye contact. I search his face for information, but he plays it pretty stoic.

"Well?" I say.

"Just read it," he says.

He walks off. I stare at the notebook occupying the seat next to mine. I pick it up, shifting its weight in my fingers a moment before I crack it open.

March 19th

This is not my life.

I wake up. I go to work at the lab and run blood samples. I go home. I read. I watch TV. I go to bed.

I rinse. I repeat.

Is this it? Is this my world?

Sometimes I think there must be more. More than what you can see with your eyes and hold in your hands. More to the universe than the physical world. More to life than just flesh.

I've read about ways to experience the more I speak of. They might be bullshit. They might not. I mean to pursue them, and I'm starting this journal to chronicle my findings. My fear, of course, is that this is another avenue to emptiness, another pathway that leads to the Big Nothing. But the way I look at it, I have little to lose.

Because what do I have now? The wake and work and sleep routine?

No. No. No.

This is not my life.

April 4th

In the past couple of weeks, I've made little progress in my quest. Wait. I probably shouldn't conclude that so definitively. I've met a lot of people with similar interests at various meet ups and gatherings, and perhaps that could lead to something. Networking is neither intuitive nor enjoyable for me, but I understand it can have great value. Unfortunately, it's damn near impossible to distinguish the open minded from the crazies from the con men among this lot. By default I trust none of them, but I don't know how far that rigid position will get me.

Everyone treats me with kindness, at least for now. It's been weird to spend so much time with groups of humans. Sometimes I forget that it can be fun to be around people, even if they might be insane.

Some days in the lab I can go an entire shift without talking to another human being. Not if Jackie is working, of course. She spends so much time wandering around socializing, I wonder if she ever gets any work done.

May 6th

I keep forgetting to update this journal. I suppose there wasn't much to report for a while there. I am now translating a book that seems promising, though. It's an ancient text of unknown origin that supposedly made its way through certain circles among both the Egyptians and Greeks, possibly Isaac Newton as well. He apparently had quite a collection of occult books and objects, and he wrote several thousand pages on the subject. Anyway, it took me a long time to decipher what language it was even written in, but I'm making good progress now.

The person that pointed me in the direction of the book gives me the creeps, however. I'm almost afraid to even write his name down here. It feels like he would know somehow. A bit silly, I realize, and yet I'm still not writing the name.

The whole Jackie thing has really been pissing me off. Three times in the past month Lemke has handed me assignments that were already under Jackie's name on the board. Yesterday, it happened again. I'm working twice as hard just to cover for her laziness.

So I decided to do something about it. I did what any reasonable person would and looked it up on the internet (Ha-Ha). I found a pamphlet that suggested I approach Jackie not as an angry or judgmental coworker but as a concerned friend.

During one of her many breaks, I went up to her and said Lemke had given me another one of her assignments and that she seemed stressed lately, was anything wrong? Mistake of the century.

Now Jackie is under the impression that we are Office BFFs, and as such, I am treated to the minutiae of her private life. For example, I now know that her boyfriend has been having issues with erectile dysfunction for the past several months. Then there's her sister, Leah, who is trying to turn their mother against Jackie. Motive was unclear.

Or my favorite, how she spent all weekend disinfecting her mattress, because her Miniature Schnauzer had a nasty bout of diarrhea.

Thank you, internet.

May 22nd
Something happened last night... I think.

It was late. I'd been reading in between chanting and meditation, which I've been at for a week based on a particular incantation in the book. At the end of the last meditation session I felt a weird sting in my nose – an unpleasant tingle. Kind of like when you get hit in the face, and you keep pressing your fingers to your nostrils, waiting for the blood to trickle out. It seemed to spread from my nose outward, but it was gone after a second so I didn't think much of it.

Over the next 20 minutes, though, I found it harder and harder to read. Not because I was tired. I wasn't. At first, it was like my eyes wouldn't quite listen to me. They fell out of focus or just stopped scanning across the lines of text, and it would take me a second to figure out what was wrong. Then, the book seemed distant like I was holding it at arm's length even though I was just about touching my nose to the page as I tried to fix my efforts on reading. I glanced around the room, and it all appeared that way, like I was moving further up into my head with the rest of the world growing farther and farther away.

I lied back on my bed and watched pink and pale green patterns etch themselves onto the white walls around me. They looked like stencils of a three tear drop shape that I perceived as three leaves on a plant. The shape painted itself repeatedly in rows that ran around the perimeter of the room. When I lifted my head, the rows seemed to realign themselves in new spots. They flowed from place to place with a bending, fluid quality to their adjustments. They were like liquid. The colors oozed into each other, constantly changing. Even when I closed my eyes, the plants were still there. Still everywhere, dripping and streaming.

The back of my head started to throb gently. I shifted my body to adjust my shirt, more out of habit than need, and my book slid off of the edge of the bed and slapped onto the floor. The sound echoed in an unusual manner. Then I realized that *every sound reverberated in a strange rhythmic pulse – almost like the sounds were slowed down. The fan in my bedroom went whoosh-whoosh-whoosh with a wavering quality.*

The tingling returned, this time starting on the top of my head and spreading down from there. It didn't sting so much like the first time. I sensed it as pleasant, like that mild euphoria you experience after you've downed your first or second alcoholic beverage, long before the depressive qualities kick in.

The echoes all around me built into something louder and more forceful. They threatened to drown everything out.

Despite all of these odd sensory happenings, I felt calm. Tranquil, even. Almost mildly sedated. I could move, but I didn't really want to.

The echoes subsided. The volume got turned down on the sound until I could only hear it if I really concentrated. And then the ceiling and walls faded out. Everything went white. My eyes were still open, but apart from the sensation of breathing, it was like I was no longer connected to the physical world. It felt like I was floating, not moving in any particular direction, just drifting in empty space. With every breath, my being inflated and deflated like a balloon.

And then images took shape in the white. A hallway stretched out in front of me. I drifted down it a ways, passing doorway after doorway – peeking into them at the infinite array of other worlds and possibilities. I didn't go through any of them, though. I somehow knew I was just here for this brief visit to get a glimpse.

But for that moment, everything seemed so clear. I had this overwhelming sense of what a miracle it is to be conscious of the universe, just to exist at all.

May 27th

As time passes, I find myself wanting to think that maybe it was all just my imagination. Maybe it was a dream. Maybe nothing really happened at all.

Sometimes I even think maybe he drugged me. I know how badly he wants me to believe in it all. He would do anything.

June 4th

It happened again. My mind separated from my body. There were elements of darkness this time, though. A feeling of dread as to where this would all go.

The walls and ceiling turned white again. But there was no hallway. It was just geometric shapes on the white. Patterns. It all flashed and morphed too fast this time. I couldn't keep up. It started blue, but it turned to red.

And then it seemed to become less geometric and 2 dimensional and more organic and 3 dimensional - stringy red muscle fibers and muted purple hunks of misshapen meat that seemed like inhuman organs. A series of such materialized before me in strobe light like bursts in front of the white background.

And then a disembodied face with no skin hovered inches in front of my nose, all sinew and strands of connective tissue and exposed teeth. The eyes seemed to look in different directions, unfocused.

I wasn't scared so much as disturbed. How could I fit these images into my prior experience when consciousness seemed like such a wonder? How could I reconcile the meat with the miracle?

The face drifted away from me, and the white gripped around it until it was gone all together, the slate before me restored to its blank whiteness.

I had this feeling that information was being transferred to me, but it was too much for my brain somehow. Someone was trying to communicate something, send me some kind of message, but I couldn't comprehend it. It reminded me of the scrolling text in The Matrix. Like whatever useful data this message might contain was being broken down into lines of code that mean nothing to me.

That's one of the worst feelings, I think. To know someone is trying to tell you something that you can't hear or discern at all and maybe never will. I think your imagination automatically assumes that it could be some crucial, life altering piece of information no matter the circumstances. But considering I was hallucinating or traveling in some metaphysical realm, it seems even more important.

Maybe I'll never-

The following page of the journal is torn out, leaving this entry and possibly the next incomplete.

feel cold when he is around. I know it must be my imagination, but...

Oh yeah, good news: Jackie's boyfriend got a prescription for Viagra, so the erectile problems are a thing of the past.

June 23rd
He knows. I don't know how, but he knows what happened to me.

The rest of the pages are blank. I close the diary, walk into the kitchen and set it on the snack bar. Glenn leans on the counter across from me, his forearms balancing on the corner. He makes eye contact and raises his eyebrows at me to ask what I thought of the journal.

"Pretty interesting stuff. Seems like Amity and I have a lot in common," I say. "And I mean to say beyond our… metaphysical experiences."

Glenn squints.

"In some ways, yeah," he says. "I can see that. She lacks your self hatred, though."

Did not see that coming.

"You think I have… You think I hate myself?" I say.

"Oh, big time, dude," Glenn says. "I don't think I've ever known anyone else that harbors such genuine self loathing. Seriously, you should talk to somebody, but yeah… Weird thing is, you seem to have a good sense of humor about it."

He slaps me on the shoulder and chuckles to himself.

"I mean, I imagine most people that feel that way are pretty unbearable to be around," he says. "But you're actually self sufficient, dependable and pretty entertaining. A self loather, yes, but not a self pity-er, I'd say."

"Well…" I say. "Thank you."

I wake in the night to what sounds like rocks bashing into Glenn's house. Thunder rumbles in the distance, and I realize it must be hail. Ice chunks patter on the roof and chime against the windows. Within a minute or two, though, it quiets down to the normal thrum of falling rain.

I lie awake in the dark, my back nestled into the couch. I blink a few times just to watch the gleam angling into the window from the streetlight vanish and reappear.

I remember what Glenn said about me hating myself, and a melancholy settles over me.

And silent movies play in my head without my say so, unfolding in my imagination like blossoming flowers. Fragmented memories I can't erase of the times just after Allie and I broke up.

The first image flashes in my cerebral cortex – through clouds of smoke at a party, I watch Allie kiss some guy she met that night. This is probably three weeks after we broke up and I moved out, after we lived together for nine months and dated for a year.

It cuts all sharp like being stabbed in the gut, but it's fine. It's fine. It's really all for the best.

Because I think for other people, finding someone new is the fun part. The novelty of the beginning, when anything is possible. It's a social thing, and I'm just not cut out for all of that.

The next image unfurls – I sit at my desk alone, empty beer bottles cluttering every surface around me. I lift the bottle in my left hand to my lips for one last kiss. My right hand pins the phone to my ear. It's a silent film, but I don't have to hear her voice to remember the things she said.

It's the middle of the night. You broke up with me, Jeff. You can't keep calling me like this when you're drunk. I have to work tomorrow. Don't call me anymore.

I shift on Glenn's couch, turning over onto my side like physically moving can get me away from the past.

It doesn't.

The next image opens up – I sweep shards of glass from the floor of my apartment, the broom pushing them off of the carpet and into the dust pan. I had woken on the floor to find that during the night I moved my couch across the room for no good reason and smashed my TV screen, possibly with a hammer. Rivulets of dried blood streak my arm like freezing rain on a windshield, so I must have cut myself on the glass. The blood looks thick, gummy. I had no recollection of doing these things. My last memory was sitting alone in the dark, pouring Jim Beam down my throat.

For years I didn't know that drinking alone wasn't normal. All through high school I did so. I had a few shots of whiskey before school in the morning or guzzled down some gin before I had to mow the lawn.

Later, of course, I realized how, for other people, drinking was a social thing to do at parties or with friends. Once Allie and I broke up, I reverted to my old ways, I guess. It always felt like drinking would quiet the despair in me down, but it only turned the volume up. It made all the bad feelings claw and scratch to try to find their way out, but there was never anywhere for them to go, so they just pulled apart my insides instead.

I barely even drink now, because it only opens up all the dark places I just want to keep closed.

And I remember trying to tell Allie about it one night back when we were still together. I tried to tell her about the bad thoughts in my head, the part of myself that attacks me and picks at my wounds so they never heal quite right, the part of me that wants to crash the plane. And she said that everybody has that, and it's OK, but I don't know. I just felt like she wasn't really listening.

So all these years went by, and yeah, I think she was wrong.

Not everybody has it. Not like this. I don't even know if she thought that for real or if she was trying to make me feel better.

And I don't know.

I don't know.

Maybe Glenn is right.

- 11 -

I'm awakened by someone shouting.

"Boom!" the voice says. "Nailed it."

Sunlight streams into the room, but what room? The first thing my eyes land on is a fire place, so I know it's not my bedroom. I pat around at the couch I've been sleeping on as though that might offer clues. Words pop into my head:

Fine Corinthian leather.

For some reason, one part of my brain finds it highly amusing to think such mundane things in stressful moments. The rest of my brain, however, wants that part to die in a fire.

As footsteps close in on me, I remember where I am: Glenn's living room.

Glenn bursts in and squares his shoulders at the couch with his finger shoved into a big hardcover book as a bookmark.

"Manifesting," he says.

"What?" I say. I can hear the sleep making my voice all deep and weird.

"Grobnagger, we've been going about this all wrong," he says. "The answers we seek aren't to be found at some diner or inside of a diary. The answers are in your dreams, and I've come upon a method that will get us exactly what we want."

Suggesting that Glenn seems a bit manic would be an understatement. I think he is about one notch below foaming at the mouth. He flips open the book and starts scanning the page he's marked, and then closes it again.

"I take it breakfast in bed is out of the question," I say.

"Manifesting," he says again.

"What?" I say again.

"Many people ascribe to the notion that there's power in positive thinking, right?" he says. "That projecting positive energy into the universe reflects it back at you, yeah? That picturing yourself achieving your goals helps you attain them. And so on."

"Right," I say.

"Well, in a sense, this concept has existed in occult writing for hundreds of years," he says.

My mind starts to wander away from manifesting toward waffles and pancakes and such. The chocolate chip pancakes advertised on the Bucky's Diner sign sound pretty delicious at the moment. And only $5.45? A steal.

Glenn flips open the book to the page he has been marking.

"This is how we'll pass that test of yours and figure out what to do next," he says. "Manifesting."

He taps a finger at the page and holds the book up to me. I go to take it, but he rips it away in a wild gesture.

"Can't you see?" he says. "All these things going on around us connect to your dreams. We have to solve that problem before we can solve the others. And the passage in this book is like a tutorial for how to use manifesting to do just that."

He holds the book up to me again, and again he rips it away to fling his arms in the air.

"Can't you see how all the pieces connect?" he says.

"First of all, I can't see anything because you keep jerking that book around like a lunatic," I say. "Second of all, just the other night you talked about how you didn't buy Riston Farber's levitating spoon. Now you're talking like my dreams are real, and I need to pass these tests to fix everything. So which is it? Real or fake?"

Glenn sets the book down on the coffee table and sighs.

"Well, that's a pretty big question," he says. "It's hard to sum up what I believe, yeah? Look at quantum physics. The math proves it's true, but classical physics can't find a way to make it mesh with its laws. It's sort of the idea that particles exist in a state of probability until we are conscious of them, at which point they become real. There have been tests suggesting elements of this dating back to Einstein. It's hard to wrap your head around, but it's sort of like time and space aren't even real until we're conscious of them. Or at least that's my simplified way of restating it to try to grasp it. Might not be completely accurate, but that's the gist, do you follow that?"

"Yeah, I think so," I say.

He better find a way to tie this into what's happening to me, because otherwise I'm afraid he's quite a bit more manic than I thought.

"So some scientists are now theorizing that quantum activity plays a role in consciousness," he says. "It's like the missing ingredient. They found evidence that these microtubules in the brain vibrate in such a way that they conduct quantum activity, or at least they could. They also proved that plants use quantum activity as part of photosynthesis. So they're taking steps toward taking that abstract theory – that reality doesn't exist until we're conscious of it – and finding biological structures that back it up."

He takes a breath.

"It's still a controversial theory, of course. The classical scientific view is that consciousness is merely a byproduct of such a complex cluster of cells as the brain," he says. "They think our brain is merely an information processing system that is so intricate that we become conscious as a result. In fact, some philosophers that ascribe to that theory believe that we're just functioning cells with the illusion of having free will. In other words, our brain functions, and that group of neurons controls our thoughts and behavior, but when we look back on it, our memory tells a story that sort of makes us feel like we had choices in the matter. Does that make sense?"

"Yeah," I say. "I mean, I get it, at least. I don't know how much sense it makes in terms of whether or not I believe it."

"Yeah," he says. "See? I don't buy that either. I mean, we already know that certain things exist outside of physics. Quantum theory and relativity already proved that."

He scratches his chin.

"There is even math that proves all matter is connected by some form of energy that communicates faster than light," he says. "Wouldn't consciousness make sense there? Doesn't that sound like the collective unconscious that Jung wrote about a long time ago? That we really are all connected on some level or dimension that we can't and don't understand?"

He takes a deep breath and lets it out all slow.

"They're still testing these theories, though, so who knows?" he says. "I mean, I don't believe any of that absolutely, but I think it adds a plausible scientific backdrop for what's happening to you, right? It doesn't have to be magic or anything."

"Right," I say.

"But all of that has little to do with manifesting. Forget the book for now," he says. "That has the details, but I guess I better explain the general concept first. You know that positive thinking stuff I was talking about? Well, some people think that's literally true. That with your thoughts and energy directed properly, you can sort of will things into being. There are even some scientists trying to study it. You've heard about those studies that suggest the power of prayer is real? Where people who are prayed for are more likely to heal from various illnesses? Some people think that doesn't prove God chooses to save some people over others. They think it proves that human thoughts can have literal effects on the world."

I don't know what to say, so I nod.

"There are slight variations, but the techniques are all about the same. Whether it's for deeply spiritual reasons or if you just want to will yourself to get rich, you think of a specific goal and concentrate on it and repeat it over and over again to yourself until it's planted deeply in your subconscious. You visualize yourself achieving it or having it or whatever."

"That's it? Doesn't seem like this would do anything," I say. Glenn shrugs.

"It helped Ken Norton become the heavyweight champ," he says. "Or so he says."

"So you think all of this stuff is real, then?" I say.

"Not all of it. Riston Farber is a phony," he says. "His illusions are designed to make people believe. Not to dupe them, but to use their beliefs. See, if people believe his magic powers exists, then they do exist - in people's minds. And with manifesting we now know how things people believe have a way of coming true, right?"

"I guess so," I say. I wonder if I could manifest some of those chocolate chip pancakes.

"Manifesting might not be anything magic. Clarifying goals and visualizing success could make someone more confident and work that way. Look, I don't know if any of it is real," he says. "But I'm more than willing to try it to get my daughter back."

"OK, that makes sense," I say. "So, for real, what's for breakfast?"

I feast on a breakfast consisting of a fried egg over a wilted spinach salad dressed with a vinaigrette. Glenn then trumps that with a second course of French toast made with homemade bread. Unbelievable. I'm sure the chocolate chip pancakes are good, but this meal is fucking outstanding. While I eat, Glenn goes over the ins and outs of manifesting.

"You choose a specific goal," he says. "So you don't say 'I want to be rich.' You say, 'I want to make one and a half million dollars by next Christmas.' A vague goal is a waste of time. I can't hold rich in my hand. I can hold one and a half million dollars in my hand."

"Might need to put that in a sack or something," I say. "I mean, that's a lot of bills to lug around in your bare hands."

He ignores my comment and continues, his eyes tilted up and to the right. I can't tell if he's examining the fern hanging over the kitchen sink or staring off into space.

"You say the goal aloud," he says. "Saying it out loud already makes it more real, more concrete than just having it in your head. This is not a dream. It's a desire. Something you can have or will achieve. Dreams live in your head. Desires live in the real world."

Yolk runs down my chin, and I dab at it with a napkin. Glenn asks if I want a refill by way of hoisting the coffee carafe at me and wiggling it while raising his eyebrows.

"Well, yeah," I say, holding my cup up.

"You tell it to yourself, repeating it over and over," he says. "You make it a ritual to spend 10 minutes at a time focusing on just repeating your specific goal to yourself like a mantra. You do this at least three times a day. Preferably six. Whenever you can, it's out loud. If you're in public or at work, you chant it in your mind with feeling. You hear your voice saying it. You repeat it so much that it wires a place in your brain and seeps into your subconscious. It becomes part of you."

I take a long drink of coffee. It's just hot enough to make my tongue tingle.

"You visualize yourself achieving it," he says. "You picture yourself accomplishing the goal repeatedly while you do your mantra. By the time it happens, it's no surprise. You've watched it a few thousand times in your mind's eye."

"This doesn't sound like magic," I say. "It sounds like a good way to focus yourself on something. I don't know if you need to chant to yourself for an hour a day, but…"

Glenn drags his knuckles back and forth over the granite countertop.

"I told you," he says. "Maybe it's magic. Maybe it's not. A lot of people say it works, and I've got nothing to lose and all to gain."

"So how you do you figure all of this applies to my dreams?" I say.

"I read an article once about dreams," he says. "A lady had all of these nightmares that a shark was attacking her and eating her. So a therapist had her imagine the shark before bed every night, except instead of letting the shark attack her, she would imagine herself tickling the shark and the shark laughing really hard."

"That changed her dreams?" I say.

He nods.

"I know yours might not be regular dreams, but I figure it's worth a shot," he says.

"Yeah, I guess so," I say.

- 12 -

I chant. It's an odd feeling to sit in a room and repeat stuff about how you're going to kill someone in a dream, but I power through it for the good of the team. I considered going the tickle route, like the lady with the shark, but killing seems a lot more efficient. Either way, I feel too dumb to do these chants within earshot of Glenn, so I make him go outside with his headphones on while I blast through my 10 minutes.

I'm in a room he calls his "library" now. I mean, it has a few hundred books, probably, but let's get real. Nobody's trying to acquire a card to come check out your Tom Clancy books, dude. I probably have this many books on my kindle, but I don't call it a "mobile library" or whatever.

When the clock hits 10:26, I cease my chant and head out to get Glenn. I watch through the screen door for a second as he paces back and forth on a sidewalk running through the backyard. His shoulders slump, and his arms dangle limply at his sides in a way that makes him look like a third grader. He thrusts his head forward and back to the beat of the music. This is one of the more embarrassing moves I've witnessed to date.

His eyes meet mine as I open the door, and I give him a wave to come in.

"How'd it go?" he says.

"I don't know what to say," I say. "It was pretty chant-y, I guess."

He smirks as he walks past me into the house.

"How long do you think it will be, then?" he says.

"Till my next seizure?" I say. "I don't know. They've been pretty frequent of late. I'd guess I'll have one within a couple of hours."

He gets a couple of octagonal glasses out of the cupboard and pours some water from a Brita pitcher. He pushes one toward me and chugs from the other.

"Probably should lay low, then," he says, wiping water from his mouth with the back of his wrist.

I nod and take a sip.

We watch movies into the afternoon in Glenn's "den." He has an HD projector and a massive screen on the wall. I think he said it was 73 inches, but I can't remember for sure. Every so often Glenn squints at me as if discerning whether or not I'm about to start flopping around. Not sure if he's more concerned about me or the upholstery on the theatre seats.

Of course, as soon as I want to have a seizure and go to the dream world of my own volition, it doesn't happen. The afternoon fades to evening without so much as a hand tremor. No shimmies. No shakes. No queasy feelings. No fades to black.

I can't remember how long ago the last movie ended, but I realize that I've been watching the LG logo bounce around the corners of the screen in a daze for several minutes when Glenn speaks.

"You think you're psyching yourself out?" he says.

His voice sounds a little more accusatory than I'd like.

"I don't know," I say. "Do you have any tips on how to

induce a metaphysical seizure you'd like to share with me?"

He huffs.

"I figure there's no use getting upset about it," I say. "Nothing we can do."

Glenn brushes his fingers in his mustache.

"You going to take that girl out or what?" he says.

"Louise?" I say. "I don't know."

"Why wouldn't you?" he says.

"Because I don't know her," I say.

"They have this new thing called dating. It's where guys and gals spend time together and get to know each other," he says. "I guess it's pretty crazy."

"I've heard tell of this," I say. "But I don't know how wise it is to partake in such matters when someone is trying to kill you."

"You just watched five movies with me," he says. "But you can't watch a movie with her for some reason? Doesn't make a lot of sense to me, Grobnagger."

"Why does everyone have to badger me about everything like this?" I say. "I don't bother anybody. I'm not hurting anyone. I just want to be alone."

Glenn leans forward in his seat and points a finger at me.

"What the hell happened to you to make you so closed off from people?" he says. "A beautiful girl wants to be around you, and you'd rather watch movies with some old guy? You'd rather just sit in a room somewhere by yourself?"

"What happened to you to make you such a nosy shit?" I say.

"Just answer me this one question, and we can move on. What's the deal with your parents?" he says. "I figure that will explain your issues sufficiently."

"What are you, Dr. Phil now?" I say.

"Let the record reflect that the witness didn't answer the question," he says. "Seriously, dude, where are mom and dad? How do they fit into the picture?"

"They're dead," I say.

He squirms in his seat, and the chair squeaks beneath him.

"What?" he says. "Both of them?"

I nod.

"My dad died when I was six. Cancer. My mom died when I was born," I say. "Stayed with my grandparents, but they've been gone a few years now, too."

For a second, Glenn remains still with his mouth half open. He stares off into space.

"Jesus," he says. "I'm sorry."

I don't know what to say, so I do the non-chalant shrug. Glenn remains in a state I want to call "flabbergasted," so I see I'll have to say something after all.

"It was a long time ago," I say.

"I didn't…" he says. "I didn't know about that."

I try to think of some smooth segue out of this conversational black hole but I can't. Glenn blinks a few times, and his head slowly swivels until his gaze locks on me. The awkward power of this is hard to capture properly in words.

We just look at each other. My skin crawls, presumably trying to get out of this room. I can't blame it for that and decide it best to follow its lead.

"I have to take a leak," I say.

"Alright," he says.

I don't think I would normally say "leak" like that, but I'm rattled pretty good. My self consciousness swells to the point that it makes it feel odd just to put one foot in front of the other at a normal pace. I have to concentrate to walk rather than sprint out of the den. When I get to the bathroom, I lock the door and turn on the ventilation fan for some white noise. I stand at the sink and try to decide how long I should wait before I go back.

My expression in the mirror looks wounded, and I observe for the thousandth time that my face is too long somehow. My chin looks like the Wicked Witch of the West or something. I stare into my eyes and wonder how anyone can look at me and not see it immediately – that I'm a soft thing that will fall to pieces at the slightest touch. I'm an open wound that just wants time alone to heal.

And even if I never can heal, I just want to be alone rather than suffer in front of a live studio audience.

I dream that I'm in a cave, swinging a torch about, trying to fight off the pitch black nothing all around. I know I need to keep going. There's something I need to get in the depths of this cavern, but I can't quite remember what that would be.

The walls around me are the color of rust and dust and blood intertwined. Maybe it's the hue of the stone that makes me know somehow that I'm far from home. This is a cave in the desert somewhere. A doorway etched into the sand that goes down and down.

I descend for a long time. All is silent aside from the hiss and periodic spit of my torch.

After a time the flame dims and burns out, but I feel my way in the dark and keep going. My fingertips graze along the cool stone.

I feel a breeze on my cheek too cold, and then I make out a glimmer of light in the distance. The descent gives way to flat ground as the light gets closer and closer. I enter the large chamber where the illumination emanates from, and I can see the flicker of the torches against the back wall. I halt in the back of the room, struggling to keep my eyes open in the light after so long in darkness.

When my pupils constrict enough, I note that there are four stone doors along the far wall with torches mounted between them. The doors have weird symbols carved into them. At first I think the carvings to be completely foreign, but something about the one on the fourth door looks familiar.

"Choices and consequences," a voice behind me says, and I almost shit myself.

I turn, and Glenn stands in the chamber next to me. Something about him seems different, though. He's dressed all in black, but he seems strange beyond that. It's like he's not himself. The look in his eye is serious and far away, and I don't really know what to make of it. He doesn't walk so much as glide across the room to stand in front of the doors. I notice there are two benches along the walls.

"What?" I say.

He doesn't say anything, doesn't even look at me, but I've gathered that I need to choose a door.

The fourth symbol is the only one that's vaguely familiar, so I move toward that. As I turn the knob, the torch lights extinguish one by one, and the darkness resumes. It's at this moment I realize where I know the symbol from. It was on the cover of the black book in Amity's room. Somehow, I know that this is not great. I want to go back and choose another one, but my hand is stuck to the knob. The door swings open into blackness, and I can't stop it.

The Earth rumbles around me, and I hear shards of rock start to crack away from the ceiling above and topple to the cave floor. I hear Glenn talking, but I can't make out the words over the sound of the rocks. It doesn't sound like he's talking to me, though.

Then I wake up.

- 13 -

I half rotate my torso on the couch and feel Mardy behind me, nestled in the space behind my knees. I give him a pet, and he pushes a paw into the air in a swim move. Gray light gleams in the windows.

I hear Glenn in the kitchen and something sizzling. Breakfast, I presume. I shuffle out to the kitchen, sit at the breakfast nook, and he serves me a plate of blueberry pancakes with sliced strawberries and the faintest touch of syrup on top like he knew the exact moment I'd be up.

"Morning," he says. "No dreams last night?"

I know that he means seizure dreams, but for a split second I contemplate telling him about my normal dream about the four doorways in the cave.

"None," I say.

His lip curls in a manner that I read as disappointment, but it uncurls just as quickly.

"I didn't figure," he says. "Well, let's get some breakfast in us and figure out something to do today. I'm sick of waiting around."

He doesn't need to ask me twice. We eat.

The Explorer zooms over the hilly terrain down by the water. I have no idea where we're going. Glenn said there's someone we need to talk to. I keep picturing myself falling into convulsions en route, jerking and flailing about on the Eddie Bauer edition leather, but this does not happen.

We drive right along the beach, the water lapping up onto the sand and retreating in rhythmic pulses. Clouds block out the sun, keeping everything swathed in silvery light that seems cold somehow. I look out over the water that stretches as far as I can see.

"So what are we going to talk about?" I say.

"We probably won't talk about much," he says. "This guy we're going to see will likely do all of the talking. If we're lucky at some point he'll pause long enough for us to get out of there."

He squints and turns his head to get a better look at something on the side of the road.

"Here we go," Glenn says to himself.

He pulls the Explorer into a little area where traffic has worn the grass down to sandy ground. We get out and follow the similarly beaten trail slashing through the knee high grass. My feet sink into the sand with each step in a way that makes the going slow enough to be frustrating. Glenn's sandals snap like someone chewing gum really loud.

"So where are we going?" I say.

"Up here," he says and points to a little cabin sitting near where the grass gives way to the beach.

It's a rickety building, the wood exterior stained gray and black by years of rain. Yellowed newspaper covers the only window.

We step up onto the porch, and at first I think it's good to be off the sand and back on something solid. The boards groan and sag under foot, however, and that feeling fades. I can't help but imagine my foot sinking through a disintegrating rotten section and getting lodged ankle deep in porch upon my next step. This also doesn't happen.

Glenn knocks without response. After a few seconds, he knocks again, and something stirs inside. I want to ask him who we're about to talk to, but it seems too weird now that they must be right on the other side of the door.

A man with sallow cheeks and a stocking cap opens the door. He looks at Glenn with dead eyes and says:

"Yeah?"

Then his gaze shifts over to me, and his eyes don't look quite so dead all of the sudden. He perks up.

"Oh, hello there," he says. "I didn't know if you'd come by or not."

"Hi," I say. "I didn't know if I would either."

He pulls the hat off and scratches his head. I can't really tell how old he is. His hairline and crow's feet suggest he must be 45 or older, but his demeanor and attire seem much younger than that. He wears a baggy black hoodie, and his hair is styled into spikes which seem remarkably unaffected by the hat. I imagine him doing manifesting chants all day to keep his hair looking perfectly molded.

"Well, maybe you already know, but I'm Duncan," he says and holds out his hand, which I shake.

"I'm Jeff Grobnagger," I say. "And this is my friend Glenn."

"Right, of course," Duncan says, feigning attention Glenn's way for a split second. "Hey, Glenn. You two should come on in."

The inside of the place looks exactly how you'd expect the

inside of a rotting cabin on the beach to look. The two burning candles on top of wood crates turned tables probably provide more of a fire hazard than they do light. Between the candle flicker and the light coming through the newspaper on the window, everything tints a little yellow.

If the floors ever had any finish on them, all evidence of it is erased. There are eight or ten sleeping bags spread out on the floor, though – some currently occupied and some not.

"Have a seat," Duncan says, gesturing to an invisible piece of furniture.

Glenn and I sit on the floor.

"There are others, you know," Duncan says.

"Others?" I say.

"Like you," he says. "Other people having the dreams."

I look at Glenn, whom I realize hasn't said anything this whole time. He looks at Duncan. I can't decide if he has a great poker face or if he's genuinely super bored.

"Not the same exact dreams as you, I'm sure," Duncan says. "But you're not alone is all."

"How do you know that?" I say.

"Word gets around about these things," he says.

It even makes its way to a stoner hut on the beach, I guess.

"How many are there, do you think?" I say.

"Hard to say," he says. "I think probably at least 10 by now in the United States, but I think the number will grow at a faster and faster pace as time passes."

I mull this over, and Duncan pulls a little one-hitter pipe out of his hoodie pocket, fiddles with it and puts the lighter to it to hit it.

"Why faster?" I say.

He sucks on the pipe a moment longer and holds it. When he talks, his voice is all strained and stiff sounding due to the smoke retaining process.

"Well, I have a theory," he says.

He smirks as he exhales a bunch of smoke in Glenn's general direction.

"Human beings only use like 10% of their brains, right?" Duncan says, his voice mostly back to normal. "We know we have all of this untapped potential. Look at how things have changed in human history. For a long time, thousands of years, we were just hunter gatherers. Then we morphed to an agricultural, largely feudal existence. Then we turned into an industrial, urban society. And now computers and the internet and smart phones are changing everything again."

He checks the pipe with his thumb, decides it's cashed and taps it against the floor. The ashes spill out, and he grinds them into the wood floor with sole of one of his Chuck Taylor's.

"So for thousands of years we barely even used language and lived a nomadic life. Now we're building computers that can process unbelievable amounts of information per second," he says. "Each of these societal changes all but eradicated everything about the way of life that came before it. Once we could grow enough crops to sustain life, nobody would go back to being a nomad, right? Nor would anyone give up the internet to go back to working a feudal farm."

Glancing around the room, I wonder how different living in this sleeping bag cabin is from living in the dark ages. I look at Glenn. His poker face hasn't budged.

"I think what's happening to you and these other people having the dream is the next wave," Duncan says. "Maybe another few percent of your brain has been activated. Or maybe it's less scientific than that and more of a straight up spiritual change. I don't know exactly. But I think it will happen to more and more people until we're all changed. Or maybe one of you few will figure out what it's about and bring that nugget back to share with the rest of us, and that will change everything."

For some reason, this particular turn of phrase makes me picture myself bringing the McDonald's chicken McNugget that's shaped like a boot back from my dream to share with mankind. It is unclear whether or not I'd be able to bring barbeque sauce with that.

"Seems like a pretty loose theory," Glenn says through clenched teeth.

Not sure what he's so pissed about. Duncan laughs.

"Was it a loose theory when it was first suggested the Earth rotates around the sun?" he says to Glenn. "That's a pretty specific concept even if the rest of the details about the solar system and the galaxy and the universe weren't fleshed out just yet."

Glenn doesn't say anything.

"I'm not saying I know exactly what's going on," Duncan says. "I just think it has something to do with our next evolutionary leap is all."

Things fall silent a moment as Duncan goes back to fidgeting with his pipe, so I decide to chime in.

"So I take it you're not the one trying to kill me?" I say.

He laughs.

"Nah," he says. "There's nothing out there I really want to kill, least of all someone like you that might have a lesson to teach before long."

His forehead wrinkles up, and his face suddenly looks more grave.

"There are some you should worry about, though," he says. "That's for sure."

As we climb back into the car, a mix of emotions stir up inside me. I'm in some sense relieved to think that what is happening to me may be part of some bigger phenomenon. Even if it's only a handful of other people experiencing this, at least I'm not alone or insane. On the other hand, the way Duncan got all serious at the end about how I should be worried reignited my fear to some degree.

"I don't get it, though," I say.

Glenn cranks the wheel and the Explorer takes a curve into a dip over a steep hill fast enough to make my stomach flutter.

"What?" he says.

"If Duncan and the Disunion people aren't trying to kill me, and Babinaux and the League aren't trying to kill me," I say. "That only leaves the Sons of Man, right? The craziest of the crazies that no one even really knows about?"

"Maybe," Glenn says. "Maybe not."

"What's that supposed to mean?" I say.

"It's not so simple as that. You're taking everyone's word at face value," he says. "And you're also assuming the couple people we've talked to each represent their entire groups. The truth could be somewhere in the middle or something else entirely."

I ponder this.

"So we're getting nowhere," I say.

"There's no harm in talking to people, but as far as I'm

concerned, our situation hasn't changed much. It won't change until we figure out your dreams," he says. "That's the key to everything."

- 14 -

Back at Glenn's, I do my chants, and then we sit around. Glenn makes martinis for himself. I decide to have one in hopes that it may somehow trigger a dream session. It doesn't, so I have another and another. It's been a long time, so this gets me pretty wasted.

At first that entails euphoria, but soon it slows everything down a bit. I start talking.

"I realized something about myself while watching the Price is Right once," I say. "See, the contestants always run up and hug the host and the models, right? No matter who these contestants are, they do this. Fat contestants. Skinny contestants. Old contestants. Young contestants. Doesn't matter. They all do it."

Glenn mixes another drink for himself while my monologue continues.

"And I realized that every time they did this, I cringed as it was happening and then watched in surprise as the host and models smiled and hugged them back each time. Like my subconscious expected, I guess, for the models to frown and pull away like the contestants were disgusting or something. And this wasn't because I found the people disgusting personally. It's because I would never run up and hug someone like that, because I would assume they'd find me disgusting.

"Disgusting isn't quite the right word, though. I don't feel like they'd retch on the spot, but it would be awkward. Everyone involved would feel kind of bad about it. I am not part of that somehow. Touching and all that.

"So I guess that must run pretty deep when you feel that self loathing on behalf of the contestants on the Price is Right, you know? You worry when they aren't bracing themselves for rejection."

Glenn takes a drink and looks at the floor. I figure I should stop talking about this, but I don't.

"There's something about physicality to it, I guess. I don't think it's just my looks, though that's part of it. It's that animal level that we don't understand about ourselves. The way dogs just know who the pack leader is. Some might test it a little, but they somehow know deep down all along who the big dog is like it's a wave in the air, and they obey that. Everyone can see something about me. That I don't belong somehow.

"When I signed the lease to my apartment, I got the same thing in a different way. I went to the manager's office, and there were people there. Office workers and some lady pushing the papers around and explaining everything and making copies and all of that. And I was a little nervous. It wasn't too bad or anything, but they had me sign and initial about 10 sheets of paper for credit checks and all of that, and the lady kind of skimmed through them with me. I was sitting in silence with strangers for a decent interval, so it's tense in a way.

"Anyway, I realized that this lady going over the papers with me put her hand on my arm a lot when she talked to me, and she touched my shoulder when handing some papers from behind me. And this relieved me somehow. It made me feel accepted and surprised about it. Not like it was anything sexual or arousing or even slightly stimulating or anything like that. It was more basic than that. Just kindness, you know. I guess I must feel like I'm so repulsive that even someone putting a hand on my arm surprises me. That almost insignificant level of approval astounds me.

"Even thinking back, I start thinking that she must have done it without thinking. Or maybe it's like a customer service or sales skill they've learned, that you can put people at ease by touching them and make the transaction easier. Part of my brain still won't accept it at face value, even though it's nothing of significance.

"Even when I go to the dentist, I feel really thankful afterward. Thankful to the point of being humbled. I feel like they did something for me that they didn't have to do. Like I'm not worth having my teeth cleaned or something, but they performed this stunning act of charity anyway. I have to remind myself that it's just a service I paid for. It's not personal for them. And then in a way that actually bums me out cause I have to think about how they don't actually care. They weren't actually doing me some favor and taking care of me out of kindness or compassion. They're just doing their job. And something is wrong with me to feel this way.

"I guess the way I think of it is that on some animal level I've been rejected. Rejected by the species, I guess. I'm not part of that part of being a human. I can't connect with other people on that level. I am outside of that. I don't mean this in some maudlin 'it's so hard being me' way or anything. It is the order I have observed in the world, and I accept it the same way that I accept that when I drop things they fall onto the floor because of gravity.

"There's no use getting all upset about it and cursing God and moaning to the heavens. I figure none of us will be here for that long either way."

Glenn slurps down the last of his drink. I can see from the lines in his face that he's still processing what I've said.

"Listen kid," he says. "You can't say shit like that. You have to-"

But before he can say what I have to do, I realize that I'm falling off the stool at the snack bar. The world fades to black before I hit the floor.

For once, I know where I am before I open my eyes. I see the alley sprawl before me in my mind before I even regain consciousness. This seems significant. Like now that I've been doing my chants, all of my life force is prepared for this. My willpower is a loaded gun waiting to go off.

I go about untying my foot and lowering myself to the ground. I walk through the mud puddles and stop at the dumpster. I can see what's inside it before I pop the lid. I can feel it.

The lid swings free, and a gigantic axe sits atop the garbage pile. This is no lumberjack axe. It's probably best described as a "video game axe." It's the ornate medieval style battle axe I've been imagining here for the past couple of days. I think I literally got the image from the cover of some role playing game in the closet at Glenn's, and now I have willed it into existence on whatever plane this dream is transpiring.

I lift it, and it has a good amount of heft to it. It feels heavy, but not too heavy. It's about the right weight to take a hooded head clean off, I'd say.

I smile.

Any minute now a hooded man will come barreling out of nowhere and get axe murdered by me.

So that's good.

I wait, though. This seems to be taking longer than normal. I can't help but consider the notion that as soon as I'm armed he won't show for the sake of irony. Or maybe he's one upping me by digging out a couple of sawed off shotguns. That would be just like him.

But no, he comes rambling around the corner just like always. He doesn't slow down when he spies my axe, which is a little intimidating in a way. Pretty brazen.

As he closes in, it's like the whole world goes into slow motion. I wind up, pulling the axe behind my head and bringing my arms straight up. The weapon hovers there a moment, waiting for him to come into range. I uncoil and everything goes back to full speed as I give him a double fisted chop to the chest. The force of this feels insane and brings a violently abrupt stop to his forward momentum. The axe blade buries itself deep in his sternum region. I release the handle, and he drops to his knees, the axe still planted in his chest. His arms dangle as limp as noodles at his sides. I give him a shove to make sure he falls on his back. I can't think of any good reason to do this except that it was how I always pictured it when I did my chants.

He doesn't twitch or writhe in agony. He lies still.

So this is it. I've vanquished the hooded bastard.

I yell a wordless scream. I feel invincible. I feel like no matter what is thrown at me, I will strike it down and crush it.

If someone dares to speak ill of me, I will pluck their words from the air and send them echoing back to destroy their master.

I feel powerful. I feel like the answer to every question I might ever ask is "Yes."

A jolt runs all through me. I guess it must be adrenalin. A tingle that centers around my chest and courses up and down my arms and legs in waves that somehow feel electric and liquid at the same time.

My breath heaves hot through my teeth, and cold sweat drips from the corners of my brow.

Something isn't quite right, though. I run back through the event in my mind, feeling the force of the axe colliding with the torso again. I look at the body lying motionless in the alley before me.

"Now what?" I say.

I look at the sky and see only gray, though. Not clouds even, just a shapeless gray heaven above. It almost seems greasy somehow. Like if I dabbed a napkin at the sky, it'd come away all orange and heavy with wet.

"Now what?" I repeat, yelling this time.

The hooded man starts quivering on the ground. His arms and legs shake about for a moment and then go rigid. He sits up halfway and hops to his feet in one motion. His fingers latch onto the axe handle and pull at it, yanking it free from his ribcage after three jerks. He tosses it aside and moves toward me.

I don't run away. I accelerate toward him, get low and drive my shoulders into his belly, tackling him. My face grinds into his open chest wound for a moment during the take down, and his blood smears my face and gushes into my eyes like ketchup out of a packet. I blink a few times, but it doesn't help much. All I can see is black blur with a ring of red around it. I feel him under me and find his neck, crushing it with my hands.

He fights at me, clawing and pushing and grabbing, but I've got him good. I squeeze and don't let go.

After a time, he stops squirming. I bring my t-shirt to my eyes and start trying to wipe clear the blood. This doesn't work very well. I can see a little bit, but I need some liquid to flush the blood out.

I crawl toward where I think the axe landed and my hand lands in a mud puddle. Ah. I lean down and scoop handfuls of water to my eyeballs. The blur starts to change shape a bit. It turns more red than black.

Just as my vision is partially restored, something heavy shoves my face into the puddle and bashes my teeth into the asphalt. I scream, but it doesn't sound like much coming from underwater. An impotent gurgle, I guess.

I buck once, throwing him off balance enough to scrabble forward away from the mud puddle and turn over onto my back. I still can't really see, though. I try to feel around for the axe, but it's useless. He's on me again, and this time his hands find my throat quickly. Maybe it's because I can't see, but something about the way his hands feel all hard on my neck reminds me of an insect.

I know he's smaller than me now, though, and I must have a reach advantage, so I reach out for his face. My left thumb gets inside his cheek, and I rip at that as hard I can. He makes weird pained noises that sound like a kid. I want to laugh, but it's hard with the lack of oxygen. I kind of hiss instead. My right hand skims over his cheek and finds his eye. I dig at that, but he arches his neck and back to get away.

I don't even care if he kills me at this point.

The only thing I want in the universe is to pop that fucking eye out.

I reach out again and my fingers brush over his teeth and nose. I find the eye and dig again, but I don't have the strength left to do much. My hand feels too far away to get any power behind it. My fingers feel almost numb, and he slides away from me again.

My chest spasms as my body tries to breathe even though it can't. My lungs burn and feel like they'll explode soon, which doesn't make much sense in a way – to explode from emptiness. This is an unpleasant feeling, but it's one I'm growing used to.

The world fades in and out in black and red pulses now. I reach out once more and get a pretty good fingernail scrape on his eye socket. I can feel his skin wedged under my nails, and I can tell it's effective as he repeats the weird childlike squeal from earlier.

I guess sometimes in life you have to settle for a pretty good eye scrape rather than ripping the eye out of its socket like you might like. Maybe that is my life lesson for today.

And then everything fades into nothing.

- 15 -

I wake on the couch at Glenn's, and he looks up from his newspaper with his reading glasses perched on the tip of his nose. He raises his eyebrows to wordlessly ask how it went. I shake my head, and his eyebrows slowly drift down into disappointment.

Disappointment is not what I feel, though. I think I'm numb to that type of emotion just now. My head is too full of flames for all that. I want blood. I want to rip out that hooded fucker's heart. I want to eat his face. He can kill me over and over again so long as he suffers just the same.

"I manifested a sweet axe," I say. "And I plunged that shit deep in his chest. It killed him, but he came back. I choked him to death, and he came back again. Then he got me."

I bring my hands to my neck to pantomime choking. Glenn looks out at the room in thought, removes the glasses, rubs his t-shirt on the lenses and puts them back on.

"Maybe we've been on the wrong track," he says.

"Is there actually a right track?" I say. "Cause it seems more like someone just wants to torture me. They bring me some place just to kill me time and again. I can't see how there can be any purpose in it."

"There must be," he says, pulling the glasses off again and squinting at the lenses. "We'll find it."

I don't know what to say, so I stare at the wall. Glenn huffs breath on the glasses, steams them up, wipes them again.

"At least you're starting to learn how powerful your mind is," he says. "I used to box, and I realized after a while that it's not physical strength that separates fighters. It's not quickness or hand speed or athleticism or even skill, exactly, that makes one guy knock out another. Those things matter, but it's more about mental strength. It's will power. The guy that wants it more, hits harder. The guy that won't be denied isn't."

I have a hard time picturing Glenn in the ring.

"When did you box?" I say.

"Just amateur stuff when I was a teenager," he says. "What I'm saying, though, isn't just that whoever wants to win will win. Everybody wants to win. It's the guy that wants to win so bad, he'll do all the things he doesn't want to do to get there. When every fiber of his being is exhausted and wants to quit, he'll keep going. It's toughness, and it's discipline, and that takes a lot of practice and hard work, right? It's just that all of that work is more about the mental than physical is all."

The room falls silent for a beat.

"Not to change the subject or nothing," Glenn says. "But have you ever had a girlfriend?"

"Yeah," I say.

I hear some defensiveness in my voice, which makes me feel dumb. I clear my throat like the defensiveness can be passed off as some kind of throat malfunction.

"Oh, OK," he says. "Just you seemed so freaked out when Louise asked you out the other night that it made me wonder."

"Well, she didn't ask so much as order me to take her out," I say. "How did I seem freaked out, though?"

"You were making this face," he says. "And then you turned all red and stuff. It was pretty funny."

"Oh," I say.

I look down at the wrinkles on my shirt and smooth them out with my knuckles.

"Anything serious?" Glenn says.

"Huh?" I say.

"Your girlfriends," he says. "Were any of them serious?"

"Oh," I say. "Yeah. One."

I keep knuckle smoothing the spot on my shirt even though the wrinkles are long gone.

"So do you want to just tell me about it, or should I pry it out with a series of questions?" he says.

I sigh.

"We lived together for a couple of years. This was a little over five years ago," I say. "Had this shitty little apartment in the ghetto. She picked it out cause she liked the way it was decorated. It had this ornate crown molding, and the color schemes were all antique. It was an old building. Built in the 1840s, I think."

Glenn interrupts me:

"It's great to hear the history of the architecture and all, but did this girl have a name?"

"Oh," I say. "No, she didn't have a name. It was pretty weird. Had to kind of point and grunt to communicate with her. Anyway, my point is that this building was old as hell."

Glenn does this move where his eyes roll and he lets his head fall all limp at the same time. It's a pretty effective display of disgust. Kind of funny, even.

"Alright, fine," I say. "Her name was Allie. Well, Allison,

but everybody called her Allie."

Glenn nods.

"Anyway, we lived together for a while," I say. "When we first met we went to a lot of parties and got wasted and stuff, but we kind of realized over time that we liked staying home more. Watching movies. Reading. Writing. So we got this apartment and mostly did that. It's crazy in a way, cause the world outside was more fucked up than ever in that neighborhood. Our next door neighbor got murdered by a burglar. The cops were around all the time, and it seems like fireworks went off every 15 minutes year round. Maybe that's why we retreated to the inside world more. I don't know. It was a pretty fun time, I guess. I still have a lot of dreams that take place in that apartment."

"So what happened, then?" he says. "Why did you break up?"

"Well, at first we did everything together. We spent a lot of time analyzing the books and movies we read and watched and stuff like that," I say. "But then I started making all this money playing poker, and she kind of got into her own things."

Things get all quiet while I try to think of how to say it right.

"I don't know," I say. "I guess it's probably more my fault, really. I withdrew into the poker world, you know? All I cared about was winning money. Everything else was boring. I don't even know if it was the money or the winning that I liked more."

I shift in my seat and more wrinkles appear on my shirt, so I smooth them out again.

"Once you get started down that path, though, where one

126

partner withdraws a little bit, it all goes bad," I say. "I realized after a while that she didn't want to have sex with me anymore."

Glenn interrupts me again:

"Let me stop you right there and ask you a crucial question: Was she hot?"

I grit my teeth. I should have known he'd ask this. Whatever, though. It was a long time ago, like it's not even real anymore.

"Well," I say. "Yeah."

"Good," Glenn says. "Good. OK, continue."

"Hmm…" I say. "No, you messed me up. I'm done."

He leans forward in his seat, the book sliding off of his lap.

"No," he says. "Unacceptable. You will finish the damn story."

"Nope."

"Come on," he says. "Maybe I want to offer some fatherly advice or some goddamn thing, right? Can't do it without the details."

Whatever. Probably better to just get it over with, I guess.

"Fine," I say. "I kind of withdrew into crushing people at poker, and at some point she withdrew, too. I sort of realized that she didn't want to have sex with me anymore after a while. I don't know if she was even conscious of this."

Glenn purses his lips.

"See, I don't blame her," I say. "I wasn't mad about it or anything, I mean. I wouldn't want to have sex with me either. But then it was important somehow, too. Like it was broken between us after that. Not that sex even matters that much on some level, but once you feel rejected that way… I don't know."

"You make a habit of finding rejection everywhere," he says.

"I guess so," I say. "So of course I didn't want to have sex with her after that, either. I mean, why would I want to be with someone who doesn't want me, you know? But I had all of these mixed feelings, I guess. I didn't want to hold it against her. It's not like she got to choose that feeling. But it was also the reality of the situation, even if she didn't know it yet. It was the big truth. How she really felt about me deep down on some animal level. What are you supposed to do, you know?"

Glenn's lips part. I expect fatherly advice to come pouring out any second, but all I get is:

"Yeah."

His word hangs in the air, and then things get all quiet again. We sit. I find this silence more frustrating than usual. I mean, what the hell? People pry a bunch of personal shit out of you, and then don't say anything? But of course. Of course. I get it. This kind of rejection is so painful there is nothing much to say about it, yeah? People aren't supposed to actually talk about shit like this, right? They aren't supposed to communicate the things that hurt them. Oh, it makes great entertainment – just the same way that people roll by a car accident real slow because they might get lucky and see some blood or a bashed in skull. But nobody wants to actually talk to me about this. They just want to crane their neck as they drive by, so they have a juicy story to tell later.

That's why I stay at home. That's why I don't fucking talk to people in the first place. Jesus fuck.

By now I'm pretty worked up. My mouth starts talking again, whether I want it to or not.

"You ever think about how pointless it is to be a man?" I say. "It's like our part in the life cycle is just jizzing. I remember this Rodney Dangerfield joke about how everything in the universe makes perfect sense, how you're surrounded by harmony and happiness… and then you cum. I think there's a nugget of truth in that. We're wired with this built in illusion that if we can just find a mate and have sex, we'll be fulfilled on some religious level or something. And as it's happening, sometimes it feels like something is complete. But it's just another lie. As soon as it's over, you can feel that. It's not even a real connection with someone in a way. It's emptiness. That's our role in humanity. Pumping out sperm. You're always alone no matter what you do, I think."

Glenn clears his throat.

"Why do you have to be so morbid all the time? Or so morose or whatever you want to call it?" he says. "Listen kid, I understand what you're saying, but you're wrong. There are meaningful things on this planet, no matter what you might believe."

He slams his hand on the end table and the ice cubes in his cup shift and make a glassy wet sound.

"It is a goddamn miracle to be alive at all," he says. "To be conscious of the world around you and try to understand its mysteries. Maybe life isn't some grand narrative with a spectacular ending like you might want. It's a series of moments. They might seem too random to add up to mean something huge, but they each mean the world on their own. You listen to the way a child describes a tree frog stuck to a window. You stand on the beach and feel a rush as the wind embraces you and tries to move you out of the way. You spend a long night drinking and talking with friends that know you better than you know yourself. You meet a girl at a party and listen to her talk and let the way she sees the world capture your imagination. You hold your baby daughter in your arms and think about how she'll get to share so many of these moments with you. And every one of these occasions is a world within a world. A little sliver of time where the doors to your imagination open up and anything is possible. You don't worry about yesterday or tomorrow. You just are for a while."

I don't say anything. I think maybe Glenn is getting emotional. Because of the daughter thing.

"But you? It's like your soul is sick from too much time in the dark," he says. "You've got to get out into the light before it's too late, Grobnagger. The meaning of life is all around us, man. You just gotta surround yourself with the people you care about and get lost in a moment for as long as you can. That's all you can do."

- 16 -

I squirm on the couch at night, the blanket twisting around me like a boa constrictor. Instead of sleeping, I can't stop thinking about what Glenn said. I mean, I guess in some ways he's right. For other people, anyway. I am outside of all of that. There is no happy ending in store for me. No family is going to surround me with warmth and love some day.

Nobody hears that, though, when you say it. It's like when a swimsuit model goes on a talk show and says how shy she is and how she hates having her picture taken, and from there it segues to showing a bunch of the latest photos of her in a bikini with oiled up skin and eyes staring into the camera with the same exact look in every photo that I guess is supposed to be sensual or seductive or something. She describes the location that no one actually cares about. (You could just say "the beach," I think. Good enough.) Do these people not realize that there are people who actually don't have their picture taken? Ever. They'd rather just sit in a room for a lifetime and die alone than have their picture taken.

Because they are hurt inside, I guess. Their physical existence is like an injury they can never recover from, and it makes it bleed all the more to have to look at moments of it frozen in time. To even know that the photos are out there and other people might see them.

So there's a difference. A lot of what people say that sounds hurtful toward themselves is false modesty. Deep down, it's just a more indirect, comfortable way of saying: "I am awesome and special. Here are like 20 pictures of me in bikini that I would like you to broadcast on television."

Some people really mean that shit, though. They say hurtful things because they are hurt. It's not manipulative. It's what they believe in their hearts.

Whatever. I sit up and feel around find my glass of water on the end table, drink, put it back.

I know all of this, and now what am I doing? Getting ready to go on some date with Louise tomorrow. The ultimate pointlessness. It's too bad in a way. You'd think that with me being quite aware that this date will lead nowhere and serve no purpose beyond wasted time, I'd be able to not feel nervous about it. Why feel nervous about something that doesn't matter, right?

But no, no. I get the worst of both worlds. I get overwhelming nervousness – I'd say it's 50/50 that I'll puke an hour or two before the date from nerves – and I don't get any hope of this meaning something down the road.

If I had the guts, I'd cancel, of course. It's too awkward, though. And she could be a source of information for us, and I can't let Glenn's hunt for his daughter fall apart because I wouldn't go out with some girl.

So here I am. Awake in the dark, twisting the knife in my wounds. What a goddamn delight life really is.

I spin and roll around on the couch some more. The blanket cinches around me again, and I kind of wish it would constrict all the way and squeeze the life out of me for real.

- 17 -

I pace up and down the hall. It's 5:45 PM. Soon it will be 6. Then it will be 7. And at 7 I have to take Louise out. Or maybe it's more accurate to say that she will take me out. Not sure.

I haven't puked.

Yet.

"Relax," Glenn calls from the other room.

"I can't," I say.

He may as well tell someone that just got stabbed to "Quit bleeding!"

I hear him go to work on something in the kitchen – running water, pouring liquid into something, opening the cupboard, closing it. The sounds echo down the hall with ever varying levels of reverb. I'm acutely aware of the way the reflections of the sound seem to shift and alter themselves as I walk my beat. I guess adrenalin heightens your senses.

After the brief stir of noise, all goes silent, and I return my focus to pacing. My mind wanders around to other moments of dread such as this. Excruciating waits before other dates a long time ago when I still thought dates could lead to something. Times I spent bouncing my knee for 20 or 30 minutes while the dentist dicked around before finally getting down to drilling holes in my teeth. Sitting motionless for seemingly endless stretches at the breakfast table so I wouldn't be too early for school and have to wait around in even more discomfort there.

"Come here," Glenn says from the kitchen.

"What?" I say.

"Come here," he says louder.

"No, I mean what do you want?" I say. "I'm not going in there if you're just going to tell me to calm down again."

"I made something for you, dick face," he says.

"Oh," I say.

I trod into the kitchen, and Glenn thrusts a mug at me. Steam coils off of the top of it.

"What's this?" I say.

The heat from the side of the cup stings my fingers for a moment before I change my grip to the handle.

"It's an ancient elixir to soothe the spirit," he says.

"For real?" I say.

He nods.

"I got the recipe out of some antique alchemical book during my research," he says. "A blend of various roots and a few… well… rather odd ingredients."

"Like what?"

"I probably shouldn't tell you," he says. "Just drink."

I start raising the cup to my lips, hesitate.

"Maybe you should tell me," I say.

"You really want to know?" he says.

"Well, yeah," I say.

"It's chamomile tea with a little honey, you dummy," he says. "I was just messing with you."

It is at this moment I notice the box of honey vanilla chamomile on the counter. Yeah.

"It will calm your nerves, though," he says. "I can assure

you that the magic of chamomile is very real."

Louise picks me up shortly after I finish my third chamomile tea. (Vomit free. Proud to be.) She drives a black Volkswagen Passat. Part of me thinks of this as a low end rich person car, but I don't know that much about cars, so I could be way off on that.

They're all the same to me. Cars, I mean. Four wheels? Check. Moves from point A to point B? Check. End of check list.

"You ready?" she says as I climb into the vehicle. She seems all smiley now, less sarcastic than when I saw her last.

"I guess so," I say. After I say it, I think about how unenthused that must sound, so I smile and do this head tilt thing that I think seems lighthearted or whimsical or some other more enthusiastic thingy.

She just keeps on smiling. You know how after a while a smile gets almost creepy? Well, let's just say she's flirting with that right now. Hovering smack dab in that danger zone, about a pubic hair away from seeming like an evil clown. I realize I said her teeth were among her good qualities, but this smile is getting outlandish.

She rolls the windows down as we back out of Glenn's driveway, and when we get up to speed, her hair flutters and whooshes around in the wind. Her cat eye sunglasses perform double duty, functioning as hair goggles along with dimming the glare of the sun.

"Do you like Thai food?" she says. She talks all loud so I can hear her over the wind.

"Yeah," I say. I nod an exaggerated nod rather than talking

loud. Less obnoxious, I think.

I bet you can't guess what she does in response.

Yep.

She smiles.

We pull into the lot of the restaurant. The sign says simply "Thai Cuisine," and it has a rose on it. It looks like a new building – a brick plaza housing a few places of business under green awnings – but the other store fronts are empty as of yet.

Even so, the place is packed. We find a parking spot on the opposite side of the lot.

"Damn. Looks pretty busy," she says.

I nod.

The nervousness builds as we cross the fresh blacktop, my stomach flopping around in my gut like a furious rainbow trout stranded on a muddy bank somewhere. Heat reflects from the surface of the ground, trying to smother us before we can go eat this food. It'd be a mercy.

I never go out to eat. I hate it. I presume other people find some form of comfort in being in a room full of strangers, being waited on and all of that. I guess it's like a social activity for them. When I'm in a room full of random people, though, I'm looking for exits. I'm scanning for a heavy object I could use as a weapon if I'm attacked. For real. I don't know how many times I've pictured myself bashing someone's skull in with a plaque listing recent employees of the month I've ripped from the wall in my imagination, or plunging the pointy end of a mounted sword fish into some poor bastard's throat.

I don't know why these people in my day dreams would even want to mess with me at this point. I can be quite ruthless.

In any case, today I will play along. I will go out to eat

against my better judgment. I'm guessing I will not enjoy it, but I shall march bravely into certain defeat like a good soldier in any case.

To my surprise, the greeter hustles us right over to one of maybe two empty tables in the place. Good timing, I guess. It's even a corner table, and I get to sit in a position where I can see everyone with no one behind me. I won't outright say that this is ideal. Ideal would be not being here at all. Under the circumstances, however, these conditions are favorable.

We order drinks. She opts for Sierra Mist. I stick with ice water.

"Just water, huh?" she says. I think she is teasing me, maybe.

"Well, you basically just ordered a glass of root canals," I say. "All of that acid and sugar."

She laughs at this, probably harder than the comment deserves.

While we're looking at the menu I scan through some weapon possibilities: steak knife, soy sauce bottle and overturned chair look to be the best possibilities, likely in that order, though the circumstances of any impending attack could change that. In an absolute emergency, I guess I could jam a chopstick in some dude's eye. There's not much to speak of on the walls near us, but that's OK. I'm confident I could do a lot of damage with a steak knife.

I order pad Thai, she requests Masaman curry, and the waiter brings the food out fairly quickly.

"How is it?" she says, gripping a wad of noodles in her chopsticks.

"It's good," I say. "It's almost great."

I twirl noodles onto my fork before I finish my thought:

"It tastes like a dish of really good food mixed with about a quarter cup of garbage juice."

She laughs so hard at this and brings a hand up to cover her mouth in case she projectile laughs anything out of there, I guess. Pink splotches form along her jaw, and her cheeks get all red. Her eyes flood with tears almost immediately.

I was being serious, though. In fact, the garbage juice taste reminds me of huddling in that dumpster with the dead dog right before the hooded man stabbed me in the sternum. Compared to going out to eat, those were good times.

Sigh.

"How about your food?" I say as the laughing slows a bit.

She wipes tears from her eyes before answering.

"It's pretty delicious," she says. "Not even a hint of garbage juice."

She reaches across the table to put her hand on my arm before adding another comment more quietly:

"I know what you mean, though, about that hint of funkiness."

She starts laughing, and for a second I think she's going to lose it again, but she reels it in a moment before it gets away from her. Her hand lingers on my arm all that time before she retracts it to resume eating, and a wave of comfort washes over me, though I only partially accept this as really happening.

So now I don't know what to think. Am I the biggest jerk? Thinking about her smile the way I did and everything? An evil clown? Maybe she was just being nice, and I'm a creepy weirdo.

Or maybe this sense of acceptance is the same lie as always, and even if she thinks something between us could be real, she won't think it for long. She will figure out how things really are.

"What do you want to do after this?" she says, interrupting my internal crisis.

"I don't know," I say.

"What does the great Jeffrey Grobnagger do for fun?" she says.

I think about this for a few seconds but nothing springs to mind.

"I don't know," I say.

She chuckles. I wonder if her teeth are getting dry with all this air time.

"You don't know?" she says.

"Just… like… normal stuff," I say. I scratch an imaginary itch on my lip.

"Geez," she says, her eyes going wide. "I didn't mean to make you so uncomfortable."

The smile fades. Something about this seems so stiff now that I can re-detach:

"Well, I didn't know you were going to be grilling me like this!" I say.

The smile rises like the phoenix. And a calm comes over me. With nothing to gain or lose here, I don't need to be so serious. The sillier I am, the more fun she will have, and that makes me feel better.

"So how's life in the private detective business?" I say. "Do you mostly spy on cheating spouses or what?"

"There is a lot of spouse stuff along with background checks," she says. "It's mostly more boring than people might assume."

"Work is work," I say. "But it's not like you're an

accountant or whatever. Look at this undercover thing you've got going now. More exciting than doing eight hours of math a day."

Her mouth is full, so she gestures her hands in a way that I interpret as halfhearted agreement.

"I'll assume you don't need to ask what I do for a living," I say.

Her smile takes on a more devilish quality.

"Oh, I know all about you," she says.

"I hear that with disturbing frequency of late," I say.

We eat for a while.

"From a distance, my job probably seems fascinating," she says. "But ultimately I spend the day digging up other people's dirt. And once you realize that everyone's dirt is pretty much the same, it's nothing to get excited about. We all have more or less the same things hiding behind the façade. And then we judge everyone else for flaws that aren't unlike our own. After a while, it occurs to you that it's more sad than exciting."

"Well said," I say. "Still better than being an accountant, though."

We eat a while.

"So it's kind of weird," I say. "That you have this case watching the cults, but you don't believe any of the stuff."

"Why is that weird?" she says.

"Well, I guess it's not that weird, necessarily," I say. "But I mean, we're here together because of my dreams even though you think they're completely fake."

"I think you're having the dreams," she says. "I just think they're dreams."

"Maybe that's the weird thing," I say. "I kind of feel like a lot people want to believe in my dreams. Even if they have doubts, they intuitively want something in there to be real, yeah? I get just the opposite from you."

She takes a bite of food.

"I believe in what's here and now," she says. "What I can see, what I can touch, those are real. Everything else is wishful thinking."

This reminds me of Glenn's talk of quantum physics.

"So you think consciousness just arises from any sufficiently complex cluster of cells," I say. "You think we're just neurons functioning to process information and nothing more?"

"I guess so, yeah," she says.

"Do we have free will, then?" I say. "Or are we just functioning cells?"

"I don't know," she says. "If science says we're just functioning cells, that seems like the most plausible explanation."

Her eyes fall to her plate. She looks sad.

- 18 -

On the way out of the restaurant, a man in a black suit and sunglasses approaches. He looks vaguely familiar.

"Jeff Grobnagger," he says.

"Yeah," I say.

"Ms. Babinaux needs to speak with you," he says. He gestures an arm toward the cars in the lot. I scour through the vehicles. No limo, of course.

"She's in the Lincoln?" I say.

He nods. I turn to Louise:

"I get this a lot," I say.

This is an exaggeration, of course, but the opportunity seems too good to pass up. I am in a weird mood.

"The lady comes with me," I say to the man.

"Whatever, dude," he says.

So yeah. This guy is a novice.

We enter the backseat. With three of us, it's actually pretty cramped, and I wind up in the middle so I'm smushed between two ladies. Better than being smushed between two dudes? Absolutely. But not that comfortable, even so.

"Hello," Ms. Babinaux says, eying Louise. Her eyelids seem to convey annoyance even though she is smiling. "You must be Jeff's friend?"

She holds a hand out for Louise to shake.

"This is Louise," I say. "She's cool."

I say this last part with that dramatic delivery people sometimes employ when they mean that someone does drugs or is OK with such activities. Lotta gravitas and perhaps a sense of grandeur. Of course I don't mean it about drugs. I mean she knows about my dumb dreams and all of that.

"Louise, this is Ms. Babinaux," I say. "She is a mysterious figure that periodically meets with me here in the backseat of her car to give vague advice regarding my dream situation."

Louise laughs.

"Yes," Ms. Babinaux says. "Yes."

If eyelids could kill. Holy crap!

"Well, I just wanted to check up on you," Ms. Babinaux says. "Things have been so quiet these past few days."

"I'm great," I say. "Everything is normal, so um... Louise is a private detective, actually. Pretty exciting line of work, I'd say."

Ms. Babinaux struggles to find words in response, her mouth hanging open a moment.

"That's... interesting," she says, her eyes flicking to Louise.

The nervous energy in the car is just right. I can't resist antagonizing Babinaux a bit.

"Yep. It would be improprietous to talk about some of the things she has surely seen during the course of her investigations," I say. "Adultery. Embezzlement. Bestialities. So let's just say she's cracked more than a few cases wide open without getting into all the sordid details and leave it at that."

Louise continues laughing. You know what? Unless I explicitly mention that she is not laughing during our time in Babinaux's car, you should probably assume she is. The

143

misshapen pink and red circles splotch her face again, and tears pour from her eyes. A less modest man might even say that the tears gush from her eyes, but that feels a little boastful to me.

"I am more than willing to leave it at that," Ms. Babinaux says. She's a little pink herself by this time.

"Well, great," I say. "So that just about wraps this up from my end."

"Yes," Ms. Babinaux says. "Perhaps that's all for now."

It occurs to me that maybe Louise's presence has bothered her more than I would have guessed. It's not like Babinaux's trust is beyond question, though. Despite her claims of being my ally, she's done little to help me in any practical sense.

I elbow Louise in the ribs to get the process of getting out of here moving, but she sticks her hand out to Babinaux first.

"Nice meeting you," she says.

"Likewise," Babinaux says.

The handshake seems awkward, and it crosses my mind that they could be working together. I think Glenn might even say that they're "in cahoots." I've never actually heard him say this, but I could imagine it somehow. Then again, maybe the handshake is just awkward because I mentioned bestialities and sort of blocked Babinaux from talking to me for real. Hard to say.

Once Louise is out of the car, Babinaux grabs my arm.

"We'll talk soon," she says, her voice hushed and grave.

"Sure," I say.

I step out of the car, and when Louise makes eye contact with me, she begins giggling again. We embark on the trek across the lot to the Passat.

"That was ridiculous," she says.

"Yeah," I say.

I hear Babinaux's Lincoln start up behind us, and the creak of the tires turning as the car backs out of its parking spot.

"What do you think she wanted?" she says.

"I don't know," I say. "I should've said lascivious."

"What?" she says.

"Instead of 'all of the sordid details,' I should have said 'all of the lascivious details,'" I say. "It's funnier, I think. Slightly less of a cliché."

Louise shakes her head, and the conversation dies. I can't help but consider the way she was quick to pump me for information, though whether it means anything or not, I'll probably never know.

I trip on the curb and stumble forward into a running fall. After six lunging paces, I slide safely into home base… except on the pavement between two cars and without a base. Immediately at the end of my slide, though, I put my fist under my chin and kind of kick my legs in a lighthearted way like a kid lying on the floor while they watch cartoons.

"Looked like a good place to sprawl out," I say, even though I know that nobody thinks I'm cool.

Louise chuckles.

I gather myself and we move on.

We climb back into the Passat and drive. No destination in mind. Just driving.

I watch the world slide past out the window. Usually I think the city looks like something that should wash down the gutter with a good rain – shattered concrete, crumbling buildings. Flush it all away, I often think. I don't know if we're in a particularly nice part of town or something, but it doesn't look so bad just here. The shadows of the tree limbs stretch across the glint of the sunlit spots in a way that somehow makes this place seem more interesting than usual. Less tired.

Usually the city seems like a dead end street, but tonight it feels like an open road. It's a nice night all around, really. A little humid, I guess.

"I know!" Louise says, and her driving seems to take on a purpose. Her turns get tighter and more aggressive. I can feel the decisiveness.

I try to get some information out of her concerning where we're headed, but she won't budge. It's a surprise, I guess. The thing I hate about surprises is being surprised by them.

The Passat whips around a curved entryway into a small parking lot next to a cemetery. Louise exits the car, and I follow her lead. I scan the horizon for signs of a business nearby for a moment before I realize that we've arrived at our destination. We're going to the cemetery.

"You scared?" she says, leading me through the gates.

"Yes," I say, and I shiver in mock fright.

She smiles. She does not laugh. Can't win 'em all, I guess.

Rows of grave stones populate the expanse of grass on a massive hillside that arcs up and up into the distance. I feel small standing at the bottom of it. Pathways gash brown lines into the green, forming a crisscross that looks like a weird road map on the ground. We follow the widest path, which veers around one of the many massive trees and then heads up the hill.

"You know anyone here?" I say.

"No," she says. "Nothing like that. This place just catches

my eye when I go by. I've always wanted to walk around up here."

I can see the appeal, I guess. It's probably the biggest cemetery I've ever seen in person, and it runs over some rolling hills, which somehow makes it seem even bigger and more impressive.

"It is substantial," I say. I sweep my arms out to the sides in a way that I believe implies immensity.

She laughs.

"Substantial," she says. "Been a while since I heard that one come up in conversation, I think."

I shrug.

The sun's descent hits the point where everything looks like a dimmed, half gray version of itself, which is heightened in certain areas by all of the shade the trees cast. A few strands of sunlight weave through the branches and leaves to shine wavering yellow light onto the face of an Angel statue atop one grave, but I can't decide if the image is more striking or strange.

"Don't you think it's interesting?" she says. "All the graves. All the people. Reading their names."

She gestures at a stone with the last name Junkin on it. Closer inspection reveals a teddy bear etched into the granite. It seems Matthew Allen Junkin only made it from 1986 to 1988, 19 months.

"Yeah," I say. "It's interesting."

Her smile fades out like the light around us. We walk in silence. I think we're both still thinking about the teddy bear.

"Isn't it crazy, though?" I say.

"What?" she says. She sounds far away.

"Somebody's baby died, and the world just kept going like it was nothing," I say. "Doesn't it seem like the world should stop when something that awful happens?"

She doesn't say anything.

"But then you realize it happens every day," I say. "Like the lady on the other side of town that left her three toddlers alone in their apartment last January. The place caught on fire, and there was nobody there to help them get out."

She swallows.

"And the city just carries on like nothing happened," I say. "I mean, I get it, but it still doesn't seem right in a way, you know?"

"Yeah," she says.

Her smile is now an outright frown, and it occurs to me that perhaps alluding to the charred bodies of children wasn't the best first date move.

Some Don Juan I turned out to be.

At the top of the hill, the broader trail forks off into two skinnier paths. We swerve left, deeper into the cemetery. I kind of thought we'd head back, but I guess not. We don't talk for quite a while. The leaves above us hiss in the airflow. It's not a windy day, but I guess there's a little air moving up there. By the time she speaks again, it's almost all the way dark.

"You're right," she says.

"What?" I say.

"The world will move on without us," she says. "But we're here for a little while. That's something."

And then her eyes are closed, and she's leaning, leaning – kissing me. And my eyes close, and our lips part, and her arms wrap around me and one hand moves to the back of my head, fingers riffling through my hair, and I put my hands around her waist and pull her close to me.

Corpses surround us, stretching off into every direction, but we are alive.

And then I think you're supposed to feel something. When you kiss a girl like this, you're supposed to feel something – something for or toward that person, or maybe you can feel something from them - but I don't think I do.

My eyes snap open, and for a moment, I watch her as the kissing goes on. The twilight tints her creamy skin purple. She is very beautiful, and she seems nice, and she seems smart, but I don't know.

I don't know.

I do not know.

My breathing must change because she opens her eyes, and our mouths detach, and she starts laughing.

"What the hell, Grobnagger?" she says. She spits my surname out of her mouth like it's an insult. "Just staring at me with that dead look in your eyes like some kind of wacko."

"Sorry," I say.

She laughs again, and she pushes herself into my side and curls her arm around mine, and maybe part of me wants to believe, but I already know.

I already know how things really are.

"It's getting dark," I say.

"So what?" she says.

A scuffling of leaves emits from somewhere nearby, and we both swivel our heads to find the source. In the half light I can just make out an older couple arriving at the top of the hill. The man sports sunglasses and a dew rag over his long hair, and the lady wears a leather vest. Bikers? Not sure.

After all of this time alone in the graveyard, it almost feels like a violation for someone else to be here. Whatever sense of security or privacy we'd been lulled into feels like it was naïve, and this place feels awkward and sort of unsafe. I can tell by the look on Louise's face that she feels the same.

"Let's get the fuck out of here," she whispers.

And so we do.

- 19 -

As the Passat snakes its way through the dark back to Glenn's, a panic bloats up in my gut. I need to find a way out of this, a way to make it stop permanently. No half measures this time. No skulking away to hide now and deal with it later.

"What are you thinking about?" she says.

I almost swallow my tongue.

"Nothing, really," I say. "Why?"

"You just look all concerned," she says.

"You can see that in the dark?" I say.

"When the moonlight flashes between the trees I can," she says.

I turn to look at her. She's right. I watch the moonlight spill through onto her skin in pulses. She really is pretty. Maybe in some other life…

But I can't. I can't. I need to rip it out by the roots. Before it grows into something big enough to hurt us.

"So how do you know Glenn?" she says.

"He's my friend," I say. It's not until after I say this out loud that I realize it's true.

"So you've known each other for a while?" she says.

"Yep," I say. Not sure why my instinct is to lie about this, but I suppose it will make no difference soon.

We pull up to Glenn's house, the Passat idling in the

driveway.

"I had a really good time tonight," she says. "You're the only Jeff Grobnagger in the universe. You know that, right?"

"I don't know. I guess so," I say.

Her eyes lock onto mine. Her eyelashes flutter and close and she leans in again. One part of me can't believe this is happening, like it's a dream coming true. The other part sees her mouth as a foreign orifice trying to latch onto me.

"Maybe we shouldn't," I say, just as her lips touch mine. I turn my head. "I'm sorry. You seem really nice, but I've got a lot of shit going on right now."

"Oh," she says, pulling back.

Her face crinkles a bit, her chin quivering. I wish I could erase these images from my mind, but I know I can't.

"I'm sorry," I say again and get out of the car.

I walk down the walkway toward that big red front door, the sound of the Passat easing out of the driveway behind me. The light from the headlights swings across the front of the house. The engine's rumble passes me and begins to recede. I look up to watch the taillights for a second.

Even when I know exactly where things are going, it still pains me to arrive.

I stand outside of the doorway for a long time, watching the spot on the horizon where the taillights faded to black. I need to gather myself before I go inside.

I try to forget everything. I try to filter my thoughts down to how I felt when I was with her, without my self consciousness overanalyzing it and clouding my brain with doubts.

She is smart and funny and attractive and all of those things you would list on paper about a girl you'd like. But isn't the true test how I feel around her?

With everything else blocked out, she is exciting to be around. I mean, she can see that I'm a ridiculous man, and she likes me anyway. This is not to imply that I like being around her simply because she seems to like me, though. It's that she can appreciate the humor in humanity without feeling contempt for it. She can disagree with something but still find likeable qualities in it. She can have empathy without either judgment or pity.

And I start to think maybe I think too much. I try to analyze and judge moments like our kiss in the cemetery before they can even breathe and become themselves. I can't shut off that part of my brain, I guess.

So even though I always know where these things will wind up, I continue to change my mind every two seconds along the way. Pretty annoying, right? Yeah. I don't feel that great about it, either.

But just as I start to think maybe I've been too harsh, I turn and lock eyes with my reflection in the dark window by Glenn's front door.

Because I guess I sort of know that the idea part of me and the physical part of me are separate worlds, right? And my thoughts can wind down these paths where I start to think maybe I'm not so bad off. Maybe my imagination and my perspective on the world are intricate and potentially entertaining. Someone like Louise could find something to like there, perhaps. I can be witty. I can be profound and insightful. All of these types of things. Maybe I'm not so awful. Isolating the idea world from the physical world, I start to think maybe romance is still a possibility for me, and I'm just psyching myself out, yeah?

And then I catch my reflection in the mirror, and I watch the worlds collide. When I look in my face, all of that positivity collapses like touching moth wings when they're still wet.

There's not a light on in Glenn's place. I kind of thought he'd wait up for me. He seemed so eager about it.

I turn the knob and push the door, but it's already partially open, so I stumble in. Right away, my feet tangle in some debris. It's too dark to make out, but I know whatever it is, it doesn't belong here. A hardened ball of dread forms in the diaphragm region of my chest.

My hand slaps and scrapes the wall in search of a light switch, fingernails screeching over drywall. No success. I switch to the other side of the door and flail my arm around over there. My fingers brush past the switch, return to it, flip it.

Let there be light. I squint a second while my eyes adjust.

At my feet lays an overturned table, its drawer pulled out and the contents strewn over the ceramic tile of the entryway. The toppled coat rack leans on one table leg, a couple of jackets still clinging to it while others scatter the area in all directions. I step forward, avoiding the shards of a smashed decorative beer stein. The quiet of the place is overwhelming.

"Glenn?" I say, calling out to be heard throughout the house.

I know he's not here. I know no one is here. I can feel it.

"Hello?" I say at top volume as a formality.

I trod over the trash pile into the living room to find more destruction. Framed pictures pock the floor, having been pulled from the walls. A photo of Amity as a child stares up at me, the lower half of her face obscured by a new smile shaped from shattered glass. The couch cushions and pillows have been slashed, feathers and stuffing hemorrhaging from the wounds.

The kitchen suffers the same fate. Every drawer sprawls on the floor, dumped and tossed aside. Utensils mound themselves on top of spice containers and cookbooks.

It couldn't look more violated. It's not my house. I'd never even seen it until the past week or so. But I feel vulnerable as I take in this wreckage. I feel like something soft in a hard world.

Who would do this? And what could they have wanted? It crosses my mind that they could have been looking for me. Then again, the slashing of the cushions might point to an object as the focus of the search. Amity's book, maybe?

More importantly, where the hell is Glenn, and is he OK?

I check the rest of the place, only finding more messes and broken things. As I return to the living room, Mardy wriggles out from under the couch. Here's my eyewitness that can't tell me anything. He presses the side of his lip against my pant leg and smears. I kneel to pet him.

I use the broom to shove junk out of the way and clear a spot on the kitchen floor to feed him. The meat plops onto a saucer, and the animal nibbles at it. This pleases the beast. With the smell of canned cat food wafting about, Glenn's cats come out of hiding, and I serve them the "sea captain's choice" as well. (Spoiler alert: The sea captain chose fish. Again.)

I'm a little worried about Leroy puking, but he evades any such problems for tonight, at least. After eating, the cats move slowly through the suddenly unfamiliar terrain. They sniff and take careful steps, staying low with their bellies tucked almost to the floor. Mardy seems the most brazen of the lot, opting to lie on the tattered couch and clean himself. The others return to their hiding spots somewhere out of sight.

I rinse the plates off, as pointless as it seems considering the mess, and as I shut off the water, I hear a crunching noise near the front door. It's glass, and it sounds like it's being trampled.

By feet.

Feet that are bigger than cat feet, probably shoed and everything. By the sound of it, it's more than one person.

I spin to face the intruders, whom I still can't see but can hear coming closer. In a flash, my mind lists my options:

A. Grab a pair of butcher knives from the floor and prepare to skewer some eyeballs. This could backfire if any of my potential assailants possess a gun.

B. Run out the back door, knowing they'd likely hear me and follow. Assuming I could make it outside, this one is pretty open ended. On the other hand, the Grobnaggers are not known for their sprinter's speed. I believe there's a tortoise on the family crest.

C. Hide. There may not be time to find and nestle into a good spot, but I'm maybe seven paces from the basement. I might be able to cover myself in a pile of beach towels in the closet next to the laundry room down there.

Maybe a single second passes before I decide, but with my adrenalin flowing, it feels much longer. In the end, I opt for none of the above. While the knife idea seems the most promising, I feel a wave of nausea come over me, and I decide to flop around and have a seizure instead.

-20-

I hang upside down yet again, the rope coiling around my ankle the way it always does. I look out at the alley through halfway opened eyes, and everything blurs around the edges where my eyelashes obscure my view. My whole life has led to this. The wet asphalt. The dumpster. The bricks. That hooded bastard, wherever he is. This is my fate.

A nagging feeling steps forward from the back of my mind. It wants me to remember where I just was, what I was just doing before I got here. I grasp for it in my memories, but it keeps its distance. Truthfully, though, I don't think it matters. Not now.

I close my eyes and ponder this. After a moment I realize that the usual dread of this place fails to well in my belly like a swollen tape worm this time around. Instead, a calm comes over me. The tranquility one feels when they are completely without fear.

This is new.

There is a peace in accepting your fate, I guess. I start to think maybe I'm even lucky in a way.

My fate may not be ideal, but it doesn't elude me the way it does for most. It doesn't hover just outside the periphery of my vision while I distract myself with a million other tasks. My fate has the decency to grab me by the shoulders and make me look into its eyes. And even if I can find no meaning in it, at least it's there. It's something concrete I can mull over. Most people don't get that. They are left on their own to drift in empty space.

I have a place. It's an awful alley where I get strangled over and over, but it's a place. I am plucked from my life and taken there. It's something. It's a kernel of significance even with the lack of any explanation or discernible purpose.

My eyes open to squinted slits, and I see the hooded man creeping through the mud puddles. He moves in slow motion, his feet skimming over the top of the water with a swishing sound, and his shoulders hunched in a manner conveying suspicion, as though he's waiting for me to spring some trap on him. I so hate to disappoint the guy after all of the quality time we've spent here together.

I close my eyes again, though, and that sarcastic feeling fades away, and the calm wraps itself around me. It makes my torso all warm. I take a deep breath, and as I exhale I feel the muscles in my neck and back let go of their tension a little bit. I inhale another big one, hold it a moment, exhale and feel that sense of relaxation run down the lengths of my arms and legs this time.

It's crazy how much of a relief it is once you finally give up. I realize the faintest smile has curled the corners of my lips. A smile – a real one – in this alley? Part of me wants to protest, but when I search my feelings, I find nothing to object to. At some point, you stop being afraid or upset about the way things are. You just accept them.

I snap back to the reality of the alley around me when it strikes me that the skimming noise of the hooded man moving through the mud puddles ended some time ago. If he were coming straight for me, he would have reached me already, even moving in slow motion like he was.

I peel my eyes a quarter of the way open to see him kneeling five feet from where I hang. One knee touches the blacktop, and the other leg forms a right angle with this hands resting on it. He bends slightly at the waist, his head tilted toward the ground beneath me, though I can't tell if this is out deference or something else. I watch for movement for a few seconds, but he doesn't stir.

The impulse to shrug comes over me, but I don't quite have the desire to follow through on it physically. Instead, my body remains motionless, and I close my eyes again.

So I hold still, and he kneels? I don't know what any of this means, and for once, I don't care. I'm content to hang here a while. The only downside I can think of is that my face feels heavy with the pressure of all of the extra blood gravity drags down this way. It's a mild annoyance, though, and nothing compared to the sense of peace that keeps washing over me every time I close my eyes and choose to stay still.

I try to remember what things were like before all of this, before I started making my periodic trek to this alley, I mean, but it's hard to call it to mind just now. I can't recall what life felt like. What did I do all day? What did I think about? All of my memories of that time seem out of focus somehow.

I struggle to conjure a clear image, but as I pull out an obscure memory of feeding Mardy in a hurry before getting back to playing video games, a feeling comes over me. It's a sick feeling. A queasiness in the belly. A sense of the emptiness that I could never have been aware of at the time erodes my newfound calmness. It's a desperate feeling, like there couldn't have been any point to living before this alley came into my life.

And I sense that it's darker outside now. Even through my eyelids I can tell. I take a breath before I look to see that the hooded man is gone, but that's not what's making it darker. It's the black fog forming a circular perimeter around me about 15 feet out and closing fast. The ebon wall of mist undulates and lurches toward me like a living thing.

I remember the cold of sticking my hand into the fog, and it sends the chill through the rest of me. And now I'm bending at the waist, fumbling to undo the lash at my ankle even though there's not enough time and there's no place to run. The calm is so gone that it crosses my mind that pissing and/or shitting myself from fear is a real possibility at the moment. An ironically detached self critique runs through my mind as my fingers fail to undo the knot:

"Am I the type to stay cool under pressure? What do I do in times of crisis?"

The detached voice in my head answers itself aloud through my lips:

"Pants. Poop them."

Tendrils of black reach out for me now, one brushing my shirt before it hooks back toward the wall. My fingers slip on the rope again, and I know it's no use. I ease my abdominals and let myself hang again, my hands dangling toward the blacktop. So that's it. I give up. The dread feels like a physical object in my stomach that I could projectile vomit every which way at any moment.

The wall of fog swells and sways like an angry black sea. It's only about eight feet away now. Maybe if this were a book with a happy ending, someone or something would swoop in and save me at the last minute, but I'm afraid it's not.

A crazy thought flashes in my head – if I somehow killed myself, I'd get out before the fog could get me, and it'd be like nothing happened. It's genius, except I don't have time to get down nor any weapons handy.

Where is that hooded bastard when you need him, right?

I get a faint whiff of a something, a metallic smell, as the black circle begins to cinch around me. I close my eyes once again, this time not out of any sense of calm or relaxation but out of fear. Wild fear as pure and deep as a child's. I can't bear to watch the black nothing envelop me. Because that's what it is. It's not darkness. It's nothingness. I don't know why I'm sure of this, but I am.

The cold coils around my shoulders first, and then I feel its chill crawl all up and down me. It starts to squeeze icy fingers at the exposed skin along my neck and arms. It stings at first, but within seconds my arms and legs are numb, and the frigidity presses itself against me like a pervert on the subway.

And I feel my breath heave hot between my clenched teeth, puffing wind over lips dried and cracking from the cold, and I know that the black will engulf me any second. It will take me. And the words "fucking terrified" spring to mind. I feel like I should try to brace myself for nothingness, but I don't know how to do that. My fists clench, but I doubt it will help.

And then it's like the lash at my ankle releases, and the bottom of the world drops out, and I'm falling, falling. I open my eyes out of instinct, but I can see nothing. A rapid descent into a black forever. I try to scream and flail my arms, but I can't make a sound nor do I get the sense my arms are doing what I tell them to. I feel the scream churning in my throat despite the lack of sound. I can't see anything to be able to confirm or disconfirm it, but it's like my arms aren't even there.

Down.

Down.

Down.

I leave the alley behind. I leave the world behind. The big shadow swallows me up forever and ever, and I tumble toward some belly that may or may not exist. Or maybe some other terror altogether.

Falling.

Falling.

My thoughts start... fracture... linear monologue... splinter off... fragments... can't follow... maybe the dark... crawling in... blotting out...

I focus hard, almost like flexing my brain, and my thoughts flow back together into a stream that makes sense. For now. It seems important to hold it together for as long as I can.

The plummet stretches on and on, seeming to pick up speed all the while, and I try to stop screaming silence, but I can't. I can't turn it off. It's like that's all I am, I think. A feeling like a scream in a throat, and the consciousness to observe it.

I don't know. Do not know. But yeah. Yep. Better go with it.

So I scream a soundless scream, and I fall and fall and fall into the pitch black nothing.

Apparently, it's a long way down.

- 21 -

I try to open my eyes, but yellow static fills my field of vision. It vibrates inside of my head like a mild electric energy and makes everything sound and appear all fizzled. My jaw clenches in violent, involuntarily bursts like my top and bottom teeth are trying to bite through each other. I can feel my head lolling on my neck, shaking and spasming along with the waves of the energy in my skull.

And then pins and needles ripple up and down my body. I can feel my arms and legs again, but I can't move them. The tingle and prickling sensations swell into full on stabs and slashes, and then that hurt intensifies again and spreads over all of me like the skin is being peeled back from the muscle, like I'm being flayed alive.

Every nerve ending is alive and screaming. I try to scream along with them, but my mouth remains motionless, my vocal cords keep still.

It's pain. It's paralysis. It's blindness and deafness and dumbness. I'm trapped inside myself, inside this flesh, and being tortured. On some level, though, I feel like the physical world is there, just on the other side of the yellow and the flaying, and that's a relief after the black nothing.

Time passes. The isolation and torment almost become a game. A challenge to endure. It doesn't scare me. Not anymore.

I'm trapped within my body, yes, but I know now it's only flesh somehow. It's hard to explain the distinction. It's like how when you're a kid, scary movies terrify you, but as you grow older, you realize "it's just a movie." And once you learn that, it's like on some level nothing that can happen in a movie can scare you anymore. Well, it's "just flesh," and on some level, these matters can't scare me anymore.

Falling into the pitch black nothing scares me. I have stared into the void, have been reduced to consciousness blinking off and on in the face of it.

But the physical plane and the nothing plane are separate I see now, and never the twain shall meet. My physical being will never experience death, not consciously anyway. So the things that happen here don't scare me anymore than a monster in a movie.

That's the funny thing about life – getting over the fear of death is the hard part. After that, it's easy.

The yellow fades to a lesser intensity over time, and I can see through the golden swells and rippled spots. The pain also fades. My limbs tingle more like they're deeply asleep rather than being speared and peeled.

I lie on my back, looking up. The black is gone, nor am I in the alley. In their stead, stone walls surround me. Flame flickers from torches mounted at even intervals around the room. As my eyes trace the rocks upward, the walls give way to an arched ceiling of brick way up there. I hold still and take it in for a moment. While the room is large, I get the sense that it's a single chamber and not part of something bigger. (Or maybe it's an antechamber. I've never been clear on the difference.)

I sit up, my movements slowed by the throbbing and

prickling. The smooth floor spans the 50 or so feet of room in front of me. It's empty from what I can see, but something glints near the far wall. I move toward it, my shuffling footsteps echoing all about me.

As I near the far wall, I see that four stone columns protrude from the floor, standing just higher than eye level. Atop each of these platforms rests an object: a sword, a stick, a cup and a coin. Looking closer, though, I believe the stick to be a wand.

I stop short of the columns and examine them. Apart from a decorative flourish of engravings along the lip, they look basically like the walls – stones mortared together somehow and piled high. The ornate bits cover the top six inches of each column. The carvings appear organic somehow, not geometric shapes, something more chaotic. Each one is unique yet equally striking.

A hushed feeling comes over me like this is important. Maybe it's sacred, maybe it's not, but I know I should proceed with caution. I study each object:

The sword rests next to its scabbard, unsheathed and shiny. There's a curve to the blade. No scuffs. No blemishes. It looks like it's never been used. The carving below depicts feathers and leaves that seem to float about each other.

The cup looks plain and old. A goblet or chalice, I guess you'd call it. It's brownish pottery of some type with a fat stem and fatter top. I can't see whether or not there's anything inside. Underneath, the carving seems to be crafted of coral and shell and shaped into portrayals of swirling fluid.

The wand tapers on one end. It's black and almost fuzzy looking with faint brown stripes that texturally remind me of scars. The carving on this column sports flame wrapping around the charred and pocked remains of something I can't identify. If I had to guess, I'd say that the charred corpse of a possum may have been integrated into the piece. For real.

The coin looks to be thick and gold. A purple bag sits nearby, like an ancient purse some king would tote around. The purse string cinches the top too tight to see for sure, but the bottom of the bag plumps in a manner suggesting more coins within. This carving looks like muscle and blood vessels and connective tissue – all stringy and sinewy and gristly.

So that's it, then. Four objects on display, though what they might mean, I couldn't say. I wonder if I'm supposed to use one to accomplish something.

Out of all of them, the one that seems to draw me in the most is the cup. Don't get me wrong. The sword is awesome, and the wand intrigues me. I figure money has little value here, so the coin won't do me much good. In any case, I find myself wondering what might be in the cup. I'm picturing some kind of kickass merlot in there. I'm not even a wine drinker, but I would take a toot off there. Truth is, I'd be happy enough with grape juice. I'm parched. Or maybe I'm convincing myself I'm thirsty because I'm such a beverage enthusiast. Hard to say, but my mouth is watering nonetheless.

I hoist the goblet, my fingers wreathing around the stem to cup the round part. It's heavy. I ease it toward me, moving slowly – half out of some reverence for this place and half out of the fear of spilling precious liquids. It slides under my nose, and I get a glimpse inside.

Not a drop to drink. The cup is empty.

Out of the corner of my eye, I see the columns jerk into

motion. The grind of rock on rock swells around me. The stone pedestals descend into the floor, moving quite quickly.

"Shit," I say out loud, and the sound of my voice startles me.

It occurs to me that I totally should have taken the sword. I rush to put the cup back on the column, but it totters and when I try to steady it, it tumbles off the other side out of view. Based on the clatter, I figure it's broken. I scramble to grab it, though, and it's fine. No damage.

On the downside, the columns and the other objects are long gone, vanished into holes in the floor that seem bottomless from my vantage point.

Great. So I'm stuck with an empty cup instead of a sweet blade.

Unless…

The cup teetering off of the column and nearly breaking calls forth a notion. If I break the cup, wouldn't this scene reset, and I could make the better choice? Just the same way that I came back every time the hooded man strangled me?

I figure I don't have much to lose, so I whip the cup at the floor as hard as I can. It explodes into a spray of shards, some of it almost disintegrating into powder on impact. The high pitched ring of the breaking pottery bounces around the room for a long moment.

And it occurs to me that perhaps this was a bad idea. Maybe I should have waited. I don't know why I'm always rushing into things.

I stop. I wait. I listen.

Nothing happens. Half of me expects the traditional reset process of a fade to black. The other half anticipates some kind of punishment for breaking the cup, though I don't know what that might involve. I feel like it could be on the loud and obnoxious side of things for some reason. A not so subtle case of pants shitting terror seems about right. Just a guess, though.

I walk over to peer down into the holes, but I see only black. I kneel and pick up one of the bigger cup shards. I rub the sharp edges between my thumb and index finger. It's about like a dog's tooth, I think. A big dog, I guess, like a Rottweiler. I lean forward and drop it into the second dark cylinder from the left.

I wait for the sound of its impact.

And wait.

And wait.

Nothing.

It crosses my mind that I missed the sound somehow, and I should drop another Rottweiler tooth, but I figure it's pointless. Here it's totally possible that the holes are bottomless. In fact, I would call it a strong likelihood.

I go to stand up, but something isn't right. My legs won't get under me to bear my weight. It's hard to explain. It's like my feet can't grip the floor. They slide out when I go to step on them, and I just stay kneeled down.

Oh, wait. I'm very lightheaded. Yep. Almost didn't realize it. That must be what's causing this.

I sit back, dispensing with the awkward leg churns and propping myself against the wall. I take a deep breath and feel the muscles in my neck and shoulders relax as I exhale. My head sinks a few inches, my neck dipping as the muscles let go, and then I take another deep breath, and my cranium rises like a buoy riding a wave. I exhale again, and my head sinks and sinks, and I'm out.

- 22 -

When I wake, the darkness is gone. Sort of. I see blackness fouled only by the light of a blinking VCR clock way in the distance.

Two things occur to me right away:

1. This is not Glenn's living room.

2. Someone is still watching stuff on VHS in this day and age. Hard to believe.

I feel around in the dark. I'm lying on a small cot under a blanket slightly coarser than 80 grit sandpaper. The floor is smooth and cold. Concrete, I think. I lower myself from the cot with care, and I realize that the VCR light is blocked from my vision for a fraction of a second as I move. At first I think someone else crossed in front of the light and get a jolt of adrenalin, but without thinking I reach my hand out. My fingers wrap around steel. A bar. I reach my other hand out with the same result. I am behind bars.

Is this jail? It could explain the VCR. They might force the incarcerated to watch Moulin Rouge on VHS as a form of torture. After maybe 10 minutes of Ewan McGregor singing, I'd tell anyone just about anything to make it stop.

I hear noises drawing closer. Muffled voices. People in an adjacent hall? I hustle back to the cot and grind the skin on my arms down to the dermis by pulling the sandpaper blanket over myself too quickly. I close my eyes just as I hear the sound of the door opening.

"Just put him in there like you were told," a man's voice says. It sounds deep, unfamiliar.

There's the sound of flipped switch, and after the briefest pause, the hum and glow of florescent lights overhead. Even through my eyelids, it seems insanely bright. It sounds like something large is being wheeled toward me.

"Can't just leave him strapped in here. Can we?" a second voice says. It's not as deep as the first and conveys the faintest Southern accent.

"We can, and we will, because that's what we were told to do," Deep Voice says.

Keys jingle. Something metallic clicks, and there's the groan of a hinge. Now the large rolling sounds seem to move away from me.

"Don't sit right with me is all," Southern Accent says. "Shoot. This fella's not going to make it through the night, I don't expect."

"Are you a frickin' doctor now?" Deep Voice says. "Stop pussyfooting around and lock the door. Last thing I want is to be standing here with you in the middle of the night. Don't you know that?"

Another jingle of keys. Another metallic click. Another groaning hinge. And a clank.

"I don't like it is all," Southern Accent says.

"Duly noted. Now let's go," Deep Voice says.

I hear their footsteps pass me and begin to recede. I decide to sneak a peek before the lights go out. Squinting, I see that I'm in one of three cells, maybe four if there's one next to mine that I can't see from this vantage point, which seems likely. The barred chambers comprise one end of a large room with only a couple of small windows along the ceiling – perhaps a basement. This isn't an official jail, then. A hobby jail? The cells appear to be about eight feet square with poured cement walls for three of the walls and legit jail cell bars for the fourth. Quite a heavy duty project, if this is really in someone's basement. There's a little office type set up on the other end of the room, complete with a desk, TV and VCR. I'd bet money there's at least one Pauly Shore movie in the pile of VHS tapes in the corner.

More significant than all of that, though, is what I spot in the cell across from mine, maybe eight or ten feet away. Glenn lies strapped to a gurney. His face is the color of the ash on the tip of a cigarette. He wears no shirt, and large, blood soaked bandages wrap around his middle.

The lights snap off, and the dark surrounds me once again. Fear courses back through me, that desperate kind of fear that only comes around when death is nearby. It almost has a smell. Death hovering close by, I mean. Not the decay aspect. The doom aspect. Imminent death has its own odor – a pathetic, powerless animal smell. The sweat and hormones and pheromones of the defeated, they smell like piss and fear.

And I realize that time and life are slipping away from me into the darkness. I try to grab a hold of them with my thoughts, like the words in my internal monologue are my hands. I try to wrangle them and make them hold still for a second, but I can't. No matter how tightly I knit my fingers, it all slides away from me.

The blinking of the VCR clock is the only reason I know

I'm not falling into nothing again.

As the footsteps fade away and the quiet resettles on the room, I realize it's not a complete silence. Glenn rasps air in and out. I try to preemptively fight them off, but it's too late: the words "death rattle" pop into my head.

I focus on that flash of a moment in my memory. Glenn looked so different without the navy blue baseball cap on. I've barely ever seen him without it. That almost made him seem more naked than the fact that he was shirtless. Of course, the wounds to his abdomen were the headline of this story. When I picture it now, the bandages are sopping wet, almost like puddles of red with strips of gauze floating in them, but my imagination might be warping things already.

Anything seems possible in the pitch black nothing. Nightmares come true. You can't see anything to disprove your fears. And so you believe them. In your mind, they are true, and in the dark, what you believe is all that's real.

A whirring noise kicks up, perhaps the air conditioner flipping on. It's a relief to hear a new sound. It confirms that there is a whole world of life outside of this room, billions of people crawling all over each other to try to reach the top of the bucket.

I lie back on the cot and close my eyes. Glenn's breathing grows louder, clicking and scraping back and forth in his throat. I try to imagine what the world will feel like when he is gone. It strikes me once again that Glenn is my friend. That he has been a good friend to me.

Is this why I don't want people around me? Because it will hurt so bad to lose them? Because all of our stories end the same way. We've all got a one way ticket to Deathington

Central.

I roll around on the cot a while before my higher brain finally slows down. I sleep. I do not dream.

- 23 -

I wake in the dark, confused until I turn my head and see the VCR clock blinking away. Glenn's breathing has changed. It sounds more normal.

I hear him fumbling with his bandages in the dark, the peeling of tape and wet sounds. I realize that his stirring must have woken me up. Perhaps he's checking the severity of his wounds.

"How's it look?" I say. I talk just above a whisper, so as not to arouse any attention from whomever is guarding us.

He sighs.

"I think I'll live," he says.

There's a wet plop that I can't place, but it doesn't sound promising.

"So who got us?" I say.

"Hm?" he says.

"I had a seizure and woke up here," I say. "So I have no idea what is going on."

"League," he says. "Shot me in the gut. They roughed up my place pretty good, too."

I hear him pulling at the straps on the gurney a second before he continues:

"Jesus. I hope Leroy is OK."

"He's fine," I say. "Or he was. I fed him right before I

blacked out."

"No puke?" he says.

"None," I say.

"Well, that's good," he says.

"I think I finally... solved my dream or whatever," I say.

"Really," he says. "That's great."

"Yeah, maybe," I say. "Kind of."

I explain all of it – the calm, and the hooded man kneeling, and the black nothing closing in and swallowing me, and the falling, and the cup, and the sword, and the wand, and the coin, and smashing the cup. I even backtrack in the middle to explain the date with Louise and the sour ending.

While I talk, I hear Glenn climb out of his stretcher, lowering himself to the floor. Then he starts scratching at something. I don't know if he's just grinding a rock back and forth on the wall out of boredom or what. I guess that's about what it sounds like.

When I finish, he doesn't say anything for a while. He just scratches.

"You're a bit of a slow learner, aren't you?" Glenn says.

"What do you mean?" I say.

"Look, I know you've had a rough life," he says. "Your parents dying and all, but-"

"OK, wait," I say. "I should probably tell you... My parents aren't dead."

"What?" he says. "Jesus Christ, Grobnagger. Are you mentally disturbed? Why would you ever lie about something like that?"

I rub at my eyes, like that will help me see in the dark.

"It's easier to tell people that they're dead than to tell them the truth," I say.

Glenn is silent, no longer fidgeting or scratching or anything.

"I don't really know my parents. They didn't want me," I say. "My dad was gone by the time I was two. I never saw him again. I guess he has a new family. My mom left me with some friends when I was six and never came back. I've seen her a couple of times since then, but it's been probably 15 or so years now."

It's so quiet in the room that I can hear Glenn breathing again even though it's not as raspy as it was.

"That's the thing, though. You tell people your parents are dead, and they leave you alone about it," I say. "That's something they can grasp somehow. Maybe it's the permanence of it all. Death, I mean. You tell them the truth, though? They don't know what to think. At first, they don't say anything, but before long they want to help you fix it. They want to help you plan some bullshit reunion or something. Like my life is some made for Lifetime movie just waiting for them to come write the happy ending for me. Like they can say 'It's not your fault,' six times and make it all go away Good Will Hunting style."

I hear Glenn swallow.

"So I just give people something they can understand is all," I say. "I don't even think of it as lying anymore."

Glenn goes back to scratching. Neither of us says anything for a time.

"Did you ever think about what the dream was trying to teach you?" he says. "Why you kept going to the alley and how you eventually solved the puzzle? Did you think about what that might mean?"

I think this over.

"I thought about it, obviously," I said. "Though I don't know if it was trying to teach me anything, or if I'd use those words for it, at least. I don't know."

"Patience," he says. "You didn't pass the test until you exhibited patience. Until you accepted your circumstances as fully beyond your control, you were doomed to the same fate over and over. It's counterintuitive to just wait there, yes, but sometimes the counterintuitive path is the only way forward. That's the point of the lesson."

That makes a lot of sense. I don't say anything.

"And the broken cup?" he says. "Any idea what that might mean?"

"None," I say.

"Wands, swords, cups and coins are the four suits of the tarot," he says. "The object you were drawn to represents what's dominant in your life right now, spiritually speaking. Cups hold water. Water symbolizes emotions. Not passions exactly, that's fire which is represented by the wand. With water, we're talking about emotions of the heart – romantic notions and poetry and our connections to other people and loneliness and searching your inner self for the deepest and darkest places."

His speech pauses a moment, and the scratching noise grows more furious. Hearing it in more detail, it sounds like something metal grinding grooves into the concrete floor. The sound dwindles as he begins talking again.

"So if a cup holds those emotions, it symbolizes the heart itself, yes?" he says.

"Sure," I say.

He hesitates to respond. I feel like I'm missing something.

"And what did you do with your cup, Grobnagger?" he says.

"I broke it," I say.

As the words fall out of my mouth, it finally dawns on me what he's getting at. This is everything. All of me. All of my life I have sabotaged relationships, I have withdrawn, I have pushed people away and looked for any reason to separate myself from everyone. I severed all friendships and burned every bridge. I broke up with Allie. Just today, I made sure things with Louise wouldn't work.I have lived my life as an injured being.

Like if I could just be by myself for a while and let this wound heal, maybe I could be OK. If the world would just leave me alone for a little while…

But the world didn't because my injuries, not in my adult life anyway. Other people are not to blame.

Nobody broke my heart. I broke it myself.

- 24 -

I try to speak, but the words catch in my throat.

"There's much I haven't told you," Glenn says. "I didn't want to complicate things."

I hear him, but my mind keeps picturing the cup shattered at my feet.

"You can lay out lessons with words, but experience is always the best teacher," he says. "The things you learn the hard way carve themselves into you deeper."

I try to focus on the things he's saying, but I have that ache in my gut that you get a couple minutes after you get kicked in the balls. The pain swells and swells, and then you feel sick in a new way, a more pitiful way. And you are just a wretched, helpless thing. And the gonad pain fades, but the sick feeling remains, the powerlessness lingers in your belly for a long time.

"You're a tough kid, Grobnagger," he says. "You might not think you are, but you're more hard nosed than you let yourself believe. Problem is, you let fear motivate your behavior instead of love. That's the path to tragedy, man. Because way deep down under many layers of denial and bullshit, every motivation boils down to either fear or love… and you're on the wrong team."

I climb down from the cot and sit on the cool floor, my knees tucked under me. I stare into the black.

"You're scared of being rejected," he says. "And you're confused about who you are inside and how that fits with who you are in the flesh. Because they are separate entities in a way. I think a lot of people struggle with that distinction."

He hesitates a moment, continues.

"Years ago, I lived in a rough neighborhood. There were crack dealers around the corner, out at all hours, and there were prostitutes a couple blocks down. Well, walking down the street I once heard a pimp chastise another man for kissing his girlfriend on the mouth. The pimp was so offended by that act, his lips curled up like he'd just eaten a wedge of lemon. He felt the guy was going down a road to ruin because he allowed himself to respect a woman enough to kiss her on the lips. He said, 'You don't know what she's doing with that mouth when you're not around.' He wasn't talking about a hooker, mind you. Just a regular girl."

The scratching starts again as he keeps talking.

"Over time, I've realized that people like that can't reconcile the idea of a woman being a real human being and having sexual desires at the same time – they can't fathom the soul and the flesh being of the same being. So to make some sense of it, they have to see the woman as an animal. A weak willed thing that is driven entirely by instinctual urges. Never to be trusted or completely empathized with. Only to be controlled. You've heard pimps and their ilk talk. They often don't call them women or girls or anything like that. They call them 'females,' just like they're referring to a dog. To love and respect a woman as an individual is to shame yourself in that world. Because all women are whores deep down. That's how they see it."

Without thinking about it, I start scratching my thumbnail

on the floor in time with Glenn's scraping.

"They have to whittle what exists between men and women down to control," he says. "They see relationships only in that context – power. That one person has to have the power over the other. And they achieve this, in part, by dehumanizing the girl."

It must be close to dawn now. I sense it's almost imperceptibly brighter in the room, but even when I strain my eyes, I still can't see what Glenn is doing.

"It's not just pimps, either," he says. "That mentality is shared by a lot of people. Way more than most people would realize. It's an attitude that's contagious. It spreads like a disease. Sometimes people preach it. Sometimes it's transmitted wordlessly. People pick up on the cues from those around them and emulate it. It becomes their idea of what it is to be a man."

He stops talking for a second, and it sounds like he's dusting something off with his hand, possibly blowing on it. Then he goes on.

"But it's all wrong. None of those people are ever going to be happy. Not really. Controlling someone else will never make you happy. They do it because they're scared. Scared of being rejected or scared of being unable to keep hold of the girls they might develop feelings for."

My legs are cold from the floor, so I climb back onto the cot and roll over onto my back to stretch my neck, my chin reaching up for the ceiling.

"Control makes you feel powerful and less afraid," he says. "But it won't make you happy. In the short term, it may satisfy some part of your brain leftover from the reptilian era of evolution, but it's not going to fulfill you over the long arc of your life. Because the deepest part of your imagination is looking for a partner. Masculine and feminine are the two incomplete halves of humanity. With the right partner, you're made whole. Carl Jung calls it the anima and animus. You know this intuitively starting when you're an adolescent, I'd say. You know that finding someone to be with is why you exist, and you know that it's not about power or control or sex or flesh at all. You want someone you can respect as your absolute peer, someone to become a part of you, and for you to become a part of them, on a higher level than skin."

The scratching stops, and he coughs. It starts again.

"I remember reading somewhere once that, no matter who you are, you sort of believe that you have secret super powers, and being in love is finding someone else that also believes you have secret super powers and vice versa. I think that's a good way to put it," he says. "So that's what you want. That's what everyone wants. Some people are better than others at blocking their intuition out, though. With the way you go on about being left alone, I'm worried that you may be one of them, Grobnagger."

I don't say anything.

"I'm not saying you're like a pimp or anything," he says. "Your way of managing it is much different than theirs. I'm just saying all that stuff about wanting the world to leave you alone is your way of blocking out what you know you want because you're scared."

The sounds coming from Glenn's area change, and I realize that I can half make him out in that purple pre-dawn light. He stands, and he scrapes something on the wall in a rectangular shape about seven feet tall and a little more than shoulder width. He turns to face me. I can't see his facial features, though, just the vague shape of him.

"I have messed up in my life. I learned that lesson too late, and my family fell apart because of me. But you are still young," he says. "Listen, I will try to come back for you."

"What?" I say.

He doesn't answer. Instead, he pivots back toward the wall, reaches an arm out toward it and pulls. There's a crack, and a white light shines through a crease along the rectangular line he drew. He pulls, and the cement rectangle shifts. He pulls again, and it slides toward him a little bit more. I realize it's opening like a door, swinging open a fraction at a time.

I can't speak. I can't move. I can only watch.

Soon the light spills into the room from the opening, and I shade my eyes. It's an unusual light, somehow unlike sunlight or incandescent or florescent or any normal illumination. It's pure white and bright as hell like that flash when you burn magnesium in chemistry class.

The door continues to open slowly but the progress is steadier now. Smooth and consistent, not so herky jerky anymore, the friction of cement on cement grates out a terrible song. As more and more light enters the cell, I see Glenn's discarded bandage on the floor, still wet with red. He turns right then, rotating with the door and revealing that there's no wound on his abdomen now.

Was there ever a wound? Did he heal himself? Watching this cement block move, I'd believe anything.

The light swells to something just shy of blinding. I watch between my fingers and between the bars. Water pours from my eyes, but I don't look away. It's too bright to see him in detail now. I just see the black silhouette of a fat, shirtless man engulfed in a rectangular flare of white that stings my eyes.

"Take care of yourself, Grobnagger," he says.

He steps into the light and disappears.

"Glenn?" I call out.

No reply.

After a second, the door snaps shut, and I'm plunged once more into darkness.

Still sitting in the dark, I reach inside the feelings part of my brain and fish around to try to get a grip on how I'm reacting to all of this. I feel a mix of things, I guess, but it's somehow more good than bad.

I sit on the edge of the cot with the sand paper blanket draped over my legs. The air conditioned chill hugs itself around my torso.

I remember the doorway into the light, and I remain in awe. Even in the dark, I can still see it. I can still see the bright white blaze through the night. I can still see his silhouette enveloped in a flash.

This raises several questions, of course. Glenn lied to me all this time, though in some ways that part doesn't bother me. He left me imprisoned here, which hurts a bit. Ultimately, these things don't conjure as strong of feelings as I might have guessed.

I think about his speech, too, and I feel some hope. It made a lot of sense.

I broke up with Allie over a matter of the flesh. I see now that I saw it wrong. I looked at things backwards. If I saw us as a linking of partners first and the physical side second rather than jumbling it all together, it could have made more sense to me. I mean, don't get me wrong. I like jizzing as much as the next guy, but what I saw as a huge rejection was really just a symptom of problems in our emotional connection, which I always knew in a way, but I couldn't see it clearly.

I let all of that physical stuff get into my psyche. I let it injure me. But that is what's not real. It barely means anything, no matter how the world around me acts. It's just skin.

When you look into the black nothing, you know how little skin means.

Nerve endings and epidermis are not the miracles of existence. Consciousness is the miracle. You can call it a soul or whatever you want. Or not. Doesn't really matter in a way, I guess. Either way, consciousness is the miracle and the physical body is just the tool to experience it through.

I lie back on the cot and pull the blanket up around me. The cool of the sheet slowly goes lukewarm under me.

I mean, it's not like leaping to these conclusions suddenly heals me. I know I'm not quite right. Maybe I never will be. But I also know that I'm not all the way fucked, either. Not yet, anyway.

And I know maybe I've been wrong about everything all of these years, at least partially. I don't know. I hope I have been wrong.

Because I think I'm going to call Louise when I get out of this place.

- 25 -

When I wake again, gray light streams through the small windows along the ceiling. It's enough to half light the cells and the office with the VCR. Apart from the empty stretcher, nothing looks amiss about Glenn's cell. You can't tell that he cracked a chunk out of the wall like a shard of hardboiled eggshell and walked through it.

I sit up, leaning my shoulders against the concrete. After a moment of silence, I hear a scuffle in the hallway and sit forward.

Ms. Babinaux bursts into the room. Her eyebrows furrow in a way that reminds me of a lioness protecting her cubs. She swivels toward me, and her expression softens.

"Question," I say. "What is the policy regarding conjugal visits in here? Is there a form I need to fill out, or… "

She sighs, perhaps out of disgust, and closes her eyes. After a beat, she hustles over to my cell, resting her hands on the bars.

"I'm so sorry that you're stuck in here," she says. "I'm going to get you out, Jeffrey. I promise."

I see now that she's quite upset, on the verge of tears. I stand.

"I'm fine," I say. "I mean, do get me out of here. That'd be tremendous, but I'm OK."

She reaches a hand between the bars, I guess asking me to come closer. I step forward, and she puts her hand on my shoulder. Her eyes well up.

"I'm sorry," she says, retracting her hand. She looks at the floor. "It's just that you've always reminded me of my son. He's 16. A little depressed."

She pulls a Kleenex out of her purse and dabs at her makeup smeared eyes.

"It hurts me to see you in here," she says.

I'm pretty taken aback by this. The emotions on her face are real, and I know I've been all wrong about Babinaux this whole time. All the half good, half sinister facial expressions I couldn't decipher were genuinely good, I think. And my doubts about her motivations were unfounded.

That's the thing about being paranoid. Your suspicions are wrong a lot.

"This is all Riston," she says, making eye contact again.

I mull the name for a second.

"The spoon man?" I say.

"What?" she says. "Oh, right. I don't know what he's planning, but he manipulated all of us into not reaching out to you all of this time so he could abduct you. I think things are about to get really, really bad."

"Sons of Man?" I say.

"Maybe," she says. "Either way, we need to get out of here. I'll get the keys and be back in five minutes."

She turns and looks at the empty gurney in Glenn's cell.

"What happened to your friend?" she says.

I wait a beat before I explain it.

"Oh, he drew a door on the wall, opened it and walked into

white light," I say. "And then the door closed."

She just looks at me for a long moment.

"I'll get the keys," she says.

"Don't worry," I say, plopping down onto the cot. "I won't go anywhere."

About 30 seconds after she walks out the door, though, I realize I'm wrong. The nausea wells up in my belly, and my neck can barely hold up my head. I lie down a few seconds before everything fades to black.

I don't wake so much as fade into being. I am running. I do not start running. I am already running as my consciousness turns on, sprinting over wet blacktop. My teeth clench, and my lips gape. My face feels all hot.

I know exactly what I need to do. I don't know why. I don't think why matters anymore, maybe.

I'm on a street I can't quite place with brick buildings running along both sides. Gray surrounds me. It tints the world like this place isn't quite all the way alive. Like stagnant water, it almost looks right, it's hard to even say what's out of the ordinary about it in particular, but it repulses me all the same.

A thought rattles around in my head just out of reach before I finally grab hold of it: This place is gray for now, but it will bleed all the way white eventually, I think. Maybe I am here to help it bleed, maybe just to watch it.

All of this seems familiar – the gray, the bricks, the wet blacktop. Maybe it's important, but I can't remember why just now.

I don't think about it too hard, though. I run. My legs pound beneath me. I almost feel separate from them. Distant.

Like my consciousness is up in my head, and those things straining and churning below me are more like my employees than part of me.

I wheel around a corner, and it all clicks into place. There it is: The alley. My alley. The mud puddles, the dumpster, it's all just like I remember it. I may not be thinking so clearly, but I remember this place.

And what's that hanging from the post? The hooded man. His robe sags differently being upside down. The reversed draping makes him look fat and weak. The hood hangs way down from his head. I can almost see his face. Maybe as I get closer…

I think he spies me barreling toward him. His torso jerks, and he jolts into action, bending at the waist to work at the lash on his ankle. He'll need to work quickly, because I'm rocketing right at him. And I don't have the best intentions.

I cover the ground between us in a flash. To my surprise, he frees his ankle and drops in front of me right as I'm arriving. He runs. I chase. It's not a long chase. He can't accelerate fast enough to get away, and I'm on him within a few paces.

I'm going to kill him. That is what I'm here to do. I knew this the second I arrived here or materialized here or whatever it was. I feel like I've known it as long as I've existed.

I attack more like an animal than a man. I hurl myself into him, flinging myself chest first and swinging both of my arms in a frenzy of looping hooks. The blows glance off of his head and shoulders. I doubt they do any real damage, but it's a matter of time at this point. As my chest collides with his back, the momentum totters us forward into a stagger, our legs tangle up, and we tumble to the ground, a twisted pile of humanity.

We uncoil our limbs and scramble for position. In the melee, my hood gets pulled down over my eyes. I drive one elbow into his back, using my weight to pin him face down to the asphalt. I use the other hand to fix my hood, my fingers brushing back the flap of fabric. It feels soft and thick, almost like a bath robe type texture. I had been expecting a woollier feel. Part of me wonders why I'm wearing a hood at all, but it can be hard to concentrate on matters of fashion when you're possessed by a homicidal rage.

He squirms, so I lean back, giving myself room to wind up and throw a haymaker with my free hand that smashes him in the back of the neck. Off balance and without my legs under me, I don't know how much power I can generate, though it seems to land solidly with a weird scrape and crack. He whimpers. He always sounds so squeaky, it kind of weirds me out. And then it dawns on me that the scraping noise was the sound of his teeth being driven into the pavement. Maybe shattering, maybe not.

I have no desire to say anything to him. No desire to even make him suffer. I just know he needs to die. It's about all I know at the moment.

I release my elbow from his back. Before he can react, I hook my arm under his throat and cinch it tight, using my other arm to lock it in place and apply max pressure on his neck. He wiggles, but he's so weak. His hands grab at my arm, fingers picking and clawing and prying, but it's no use.

And I lean back a little, trying to make it end quicker. And he stops scratching at my arm. He taps it. Like this is a gentlemanly battle, and he can tap out. Like he can just ask me to stop. Something about it bugs me, makes it feel more real.

He keeps on tapping and tapping.

My arm starts shaking from the strain. My breath heaves through my teeth, little flecks of spit traveling with it. The skin on my face weeps sweat that feels like hot grease. It clings to my flesh in little puddles.

The taps slow down. They grow softer. Soon he's just barely making contact, more like caresses that tickle than a guy fighting for his life. Again, this disturbs me. I wonder, for a second, if he ever had these doubts when he was killing me. Did he ever hesitate? Did he feel any pity for me?

I realize that the taps on my arm stopped some time ago. I release my grip, and the body slumps to the ground. I sit back for a moment, trying to catch my breath.

With the deed done, my thoughts tangle and circle around themselves. I feel no satisfaction. I guess I don't know what to feel.

I sit back, my shoulders colliding with the brick wall behind me and propping me up there. I dab my fingers at the oily patches of sweat on my forehead. There's no relief from the heat I feel.

It suddenly seems a lot more important to consider why I was so hell bent on doing this, but I can think of no good reason. Are there holes in my memories? Was there ever a real reason? I know this man killed me many times over, but this place isn't normal. Things work differently here.

Without standing up, I scuttle over to the body. He lies face down, the fabric of the robe fanned out from the corpse in a way that makes him look tiny. There's almost a feminine quality to the textile encased silhouette of the waist and hips.

I reach a hand toward the shoulder, hesitating for a

moment, my hand floating there just short of my enemy's empty shell. I clench and unclench my fist.

I'm not scared, exactly. I don't wonder if he'll come back this time. I know he won't. Something else makes me pause.

Finally, I grip the shoulder and turn the body over. The hood is pulled down over the head. It takes me a few tries to get a hold of it and unsheathe the face.

At first, I only see the eyes. A twisted web of red covers what were once the whites. The words "petechial hemorrhage" pop into my head, I guess a remnant from some murder of the week TV show. Looking close, it almost appears to be little scarlet vines crisscrossing around the iris, each one with a distinct width and sense of texture.

I let the focus of my vision zoom out after a second, and I feel a tightness in my chest. It's her. Soot scuffs her cheek bones and all around her open mouth, her top teeth sheared off in an almost perfectly straight line all the way across, cleaved on the asphalt, a few shards of broken tooth stuck to her tongue. The injuries and the blank look in her eyes make her seem different, but there's no doubt. It's Amity.

The good news is that I've found Glenn's daughter. The bad news...

The shock constricts my chest so I can't breathe. I try to remember. I try to think back on all of our encounters here in this alley. Was it her all along? I remember all of the high pitched sounds, realizing that the hooded figure was smaller than me, the youthful look to the chin and mouth. I think it was always Amity choking me out.

Did she have the same feeling I did upon arriving this time? Some sense of duty regarding the task of murdering me? Some undeniable drive to do so?

I scoot back, my hand curling to my mouth. I run my knuckles back and forth across my lips. The questions keep coming to me:

Will this reset for her like it did for me? Will she come back someplace else?

And then the gray sky above me dims to black, all the light draining away and away to pitch black nothing, holding me in darkness for what seems like a long time. And just when I think I'm about to be transported somewhere else, the illumination fades back in, the light opening the dark up to reveal the alley once more.

But just as the light gets back to full strength, the dimming begins again. Bright to dim to dark to nothing. The alley fades away, and the black is everywhere. It's everything. And I realize that I'm holding my breath, and I'm almost afraid to breathe, afraid to do anything in the dark.

The light blooms, though, and the brick walls and asphalt and dumpster reform. The world becomes something solid around me once more.

I almost go into a trance as it continues. I feel so numb, so frozen.

The sky dims and brightens, dims and brightens – the dark growing darker with the progression, the light surprising me a little more each time it returns. It pulses everywhere – light to dark to light to dark. Every time the black comes, it's like the nothing surrounds me again. The world vanishes into oblivion. The free fall into blackness seems poised to commence, and then the street and buildings rematerialize around me as the light comes back up like everything is normal.

I crawl to the brick wall and droop against it, just to lean on something solid. The alley inhales and exhales the light, and I feel like I'm bobbing in and out of water, thrust into the cold and dark and returned to the bright repeatedly.

Electricity vibrates all through me when the light comes up. I feel the jolt of current in my head, and I imagine the clump of damaged neurons misfiring in unison to cause the seizures that bring me here. The grand mal sizzle of a bunch of bad connections that I follow down to this place.

Noise builds in my ears, a growl of static. It sounds like heavy machines operating, but distorted somehow, crunchy with a bassy hum. It keeps getting louder and louder, the growl growing more and more furious. I feel it closing in on me, shaking me, rattling my sternum harder and harder.

And the dim comes. And the dark stays too long this time. It holds and holds. And it wraps itself around me, all frozen and dead. And I try to yell, but I feel the dark billow into my mouth like cold smoke and almost immediately congeal into something heavier and wet like a greasy mucus. And the slime cuts off my breath as the cold oozes down my throat and spreads over all of me. And all I can do is gag for breath and listen to the growl.

But the light comes back up, and there's a creaking gasp as the bright vacuums the black smoke out of my lungs. For a second, I feel weirdly empty and a little overwhelmed to see the buildings take shape around me once again. I blink rapidly, my eyes watering a bit. Running crosses my mind, but I know it'd be no use.

I take deep breaths, bracing myself for the dark to return. My fingernails claw into the asphalt like that could somehow anchor me here in the solid world of the light.

The illumination wavers a few times and steadies itself, holding longer than it should. I wait for the worst, my eyes narrowed to half slits.

The dark doesn't come, though. The light holds it at bay. Soon, the growling sound recedes like the slow fade out at the end of a song.

So I lie on my back, taking in this world from my vantage point in the alley, looking up at the buildings that reach out for the sky above. Light shines down from the heavens, a gray light that I don't believe cares much for me, but it vanquishes the dark for now, and that's good enough. Within a few seconds, the growl is gone completely. My breathing slows, progressing toward normal. I watch the sky. The gray mass above me that's not quite like a cloud hovers there, strands of it drifting in slow motion like wispy tentacles.

For a long, silent moment, I stare into the gray.

And then light bursts out of everywhere. It explodes from the brick walls. It erupts from the clouds. It flares. It surges. It ruptures my chest and gushes out of me. Without thinking, I bring my hands to my punctured abdomen, but they disintegrate into light as soon as they cross the beam.

And the bright swells and swells and swells until everything is white light.

- BLED WHITE -

Bled White (Awake in the Dark #2) is now available on Amazon.

- COME PARTY WITH US -

We're loners. Rebels. But much to our surprise, the most kickass part of writing has been connecting with our readers. From time to time, we send out newsletters with giveaways, special offers, and juicy details on new releases.

Sign up for our mailing list at:
http://ltvargus.com/mailing-list/

- SPREAD THE WORD -

Thank you for reading! We'd be very grateful if you could take a few minutes to review it on Amazon.com.

How grateful? Eternally. Even when we are old and dead and have turned into ghosts, we will be thinking fondly of you and your kind words. The most powerful way to bring our books to the attention of other people is through the honest reviews from readers like you.

- ABOUT THE AUTHORS -

Tim McBain writes because life is short, and he wants to make something awesome before he dies. Additionally, he likes to move it, move it.

You can connect with Tim on Twitter at @realtimmcbain or via email at tim@timmcbain.com.

L.T. Vargus grew up in Hell, Michigan, which is a lot smaller, quieter, and less fiery than one might imagine. When not click-clacking away at the keyboard, she can be found sewing, fantasizing about food, and rotting her brain in front of the TV.

If you want to wax poetic about pizza or cats, you can contact L.T. (the L is for Lex) at ltvargus9@gmail.com or on Twitter @ltvargus.

TimMcBain.com
LTVargus.com